The forest echoed with gunshots...

Abruptly Evan switched off the headlights of his car. "Get down!" he shouted to his passenger, Cecilia. She ducked behind the dashboard just as she felt the car swerve wildly. A bullet hit home, shattering the windshield.

"A poacher," Evan said curtly. "It was just a poacher, firing blindly."

Then another shot rang out. Terrified, Cecilia clutched at Evan's powerful torso. She suddenly realized that she trusted him...even though he was lying to her.

Other

MYSTIQUE BOOKS

by CORIOLA

Cruel Betrayal

by CORIOLA

 MYSTIQUE BOOKS

TORONTO·LONDON·NEW YORK

HAMBURG·AMSTERDAM·STOCKHOLM

CRUEL BETRAYAL/first published October 1981

Chapter 1

The cabin was nearly empty as the train lurched forward to complete the final leg of its journey. Night had fallen long before most of the passengers disembarked at Exeter, but the lively voices of people looking forward to a summer weekend in the country had kept the atmosphere bright and cheerful. Now, nearly two hundred miles from London, sitting in a silent cabin with only the black of night showing through the train windows, Cecilia Bennett allowed herself to feel the apprehension she had successfully avoided for the past twenty-four hours. She admitted to herself that she was completely alone, ignorant of the ways of England and hurtling through the night, possibly toward disaster.

Cecilia shifted uncomfortably in her new navy blue linen suit. This was no time for self-doubt, she told herself. She had made her decision, and the only way she was going to build a future for herself was by taking some risks. After all, she had known danger most of her

life. But that had been a different kind of danger. . . .
And now she could not keep her thoughts from slipping
back to the events of the past several weeks, events that
had left her no choice about whether or not to board
this train.

THE WALK FROM the subway to her modest hotel the
previous afternoon had seemed much longer than usual
as Cecilia returned from her eleventh failed job interview. Her gloom didn't stem from the fact that she
hadn't got the job; no, it was that this latest failure
seemed to fit the pattern so perfectly. And she had
drawn the only logical conclusion: she was un-
employable.

Miserable, Cecilia decided to treat herself to tea—the
lovely English version of tea wherein the word refers not
only to a hot drink but equally well to currant-laced
scones and warm buttery crumpets. Even the thought of
the refreshment made her feel better, and when she
pushed open the glass door of the café not far from her
hotel, she was pleased to see Polly, the café owner's
wife. The old woman loved to talk with the customers
and was capable of finding humor in anything.

"Miss Bennett, how lovely to see you," Polly beamed
from behind the counter. "Now, what can I fix to put
some cheer back into that pretty face?"

"Extra butter," Cecilia answered unhappily.

The plump old lady nodded knowingly. "A pot of tea
and some fresh hot crumpets with extra butter, on the
way." She turned to pull a cup and saucer off the shelf
behind the counter, then peeked over her shoulder at the
dejected Cecilia. "Will you be wantin' a job on the

side, to go with that order?" she asked good-naturedly.

Cecilia couldn't help but laugh. "Oh, Polly, you know me too well. You're right; I was turned down again."

"Well, it's about time I had a spot of tea myself, givin' us just the opportunity to talk, for as sure as the trains run into Paddington Station, you need to blow off a bit of steam."

Cecilia watched as Polly's expert hands prepared her crumpets, thinking it would be good to vent some of her frustrations by having a talk with the kind old woman—even though Polly was powerless to help her.

"So, what was it this time?" the old lady asked cheerfully as she walked around the counter and took a seat beside Cecilia.

"Governess to two little brats in Belgravia," Cecilia replied after she'd savored the first bite of her crumpet. "Boys, eight and eleven years old. The pride and joy of a bored mother and a pompous father." Cecilia took a sip of tea before providing the crucial ending of her story. "The answer was the same as the last 'governess rejection' I got: 'Very sorry, dear, but you're roughly a hundred years out-of-date. Young ladies of grace and poise are no longer in demand. And your prodigious knowledge of history and literature, fluency in French and German, as well as your understanding of differing cultures simply can't outweigh your lack of a degree in child psychology.'"

The old woman chuckled. "How many does that make?" she asked, reaching over the counter to raid a plate of jam-topped butter cookies.

"How many what?" Cecilia said. "Failed governess

applications or failed applications in general?" She looked regretfully at her empty plate. How had she managed to finish the crumpets and talk at the same time?

"Both!" exclaimed Poly with her mouth full.

"Eleven interviews in all," Cecilia answered. "Three of them for governess positions."

"Pity," said the old lady, shaking her head.

"Indeed," agreed Cecilia. "I never realized what a hopeless case I am until I came to London. I'm too out-dated to be a governess and I can't type. Worse, I don't have any work experience except for managing a fifty-thousand-acre game preserve with my father in Kenya." Cecilia sighed, then smiled tightly. "Do you know of any openings for young women who specialize in elephants, lions and antelopes—and who are expert riders?" she asked.

Polly was so choked with laughter that she barely made it around the counter to wait on the postman who had just come in.

"A cup of your lovely tea, Polly, to take along my route," the man called from the register at the end of the counter. "And what's got into you?"

"Oh, I'm just havin' a spot of tea with..." Polly began, valiantly trying to compose herself. "Miss Bennett's job huntin' 'bout got me played out for the day," she finished.

"Bennett?" inquired the postman.

Cecilia looked up at the sound of her name. "I'm Cecilia Bennett," she offered. If the man had a letter for her, it could only have come from one place, she thought excitedly.

"Aha," said the postman. "I wondered who that fancy letter could be for." He reached into his leather satchel. "I know most all the folks on my route, you see—even those what gets letters at the hotels along this strip."

Cecilia's anticipation grew as she watched him sort through a hefty stack of mail. She held her breath. This letter might be her last chance. . . .

"Here it is," the man announced with satisfaction. "Glad not to have to send it to the dead-letter office; this letter looks important." ·

"I hope you're right about that," Cecilia responded. She took the letter eagerly but was instantly awed by its elegant appearance.

Polly set a plastic cup of hot tea on the counter, and when the postman had paid for it he headed toward the door. "Thank you," Cecilia called out to him, then turned her attention once more to the letter.

The envelope was a pale gray blue with a rich linen finish and an elaborate watermark. Cecilia squinted at the watermark. Then, turning the letter over, she was amazed to find a heavy seal of steel-blue wax. Her slender fingers played over the intricate impressions in the wax as she stared wonderingly at the letter.

Suddenly Cecilia became conscious of Polly's heavy breathing just inches from her face. Before she could look up, a sharp slender knife was thrust into her field of vision.

"Well, open it!" Polly ordered.

Cecilia jumped back slightly from the gleam of the knife, acutely aware of Polly's burning curiosity.

Resigned to opening the letter in the old woman's company, Cecilia made a careful slit in the side of the envelope. Hastily she scanned the short handwritten message, but when she had finished reading she was filled with confusion.

"Well, what does it say?" Polly demanded.

Cecilia spread the letter out on a clean space on the counter, hoping the old woman would not feel drawn to hold it with her eternally buttery hands. But Polly stood well back from the letter, squinted and began to read. Cecilia now read each word of the letter carefully.

The Honorable Evan Cedric-Browne
Chesterton Manor

16 June

Dear Miss Bennett,

Your application arrived and appears to be in order. Please be so kind as to take the 5:10 P.M. train for Dartmouth, leaving from King's Cross Station. I will be awaiting you at the station Friday evening, June 18. To recognize me, look for a rather tall, dark-haired man wearing a tan trench coat and carrying a large cordovan case. Your duties at Chesterton Manor, which we can discuss upon your arrival, will begin on Tuesday, June 22.

Sincerely,
Evan Cedric-Browne

"Whew!" exclaimed Polly. "I don't know what 'your duties' are, Miss Bennett, but I can tell you that the 'Honorable' in that man's name means he's some kind of mucky-muck—and besides that, 'rather tall' and 'dark-haired' doesn't sound so bad, either!"

Cecilia only continued to stare at the letter. She didn't know whether to be thrilled or insulted. On the one hand, she had a job. On the other hand, Mr. Evan Cedric-Browne's 'offer' was less than informative.

"June 18 is tomorrow!" Polly chirped. She tapped the date on the greasy bank calendar hanging on the wall behind her.

Cecilia was alarmed when she realized that Polly was right. "Oh, Polly," she groaned, "I just don't know. I responded to an advertisement in the newspaper when I first arrived in London weeks ago. I never expected to get an answer, I don't have any experience as a tour guide! That's what the job involves—being a tour guide at Chesterton Manor. All the listing said was that the applicants had to be at least twenty-one years of age, personable and well-spoken. Room and board will be provided at the manor, and employment is guaranteed until October 31—'pending satisfactory performance.'"

"So what's the problem? You've got a job and prob'ly a fine lot of mucky-mucks—the Cedric-Browne family—to share a castle with."

"This letter doesn't say anything about a family, Polly," Cecilia corrected sharply. "In fact, that's just the problem: this letter barely tells me anything! There must have been scores of applicants, so why did I, of all people, get the job? And how can I decide if I should even take it? 'Room and board' may mean some garret where I can't even stand up, and a little plate of leftovers once a day!"

"Now, now," soothed Polly. "Don't be ridiculous.

Nobody who's got paper like that there to write a letter on would stick you in an attic!"

"Nobody who's half-polite would expect me to travel all the way to Dartmouth on twenty-four hours' notice," Cecilia challenged.

Polly wiped her hands reflectively on her apron. "Well," she said, "you've got a job now, and I'll be offering you no more sympathy if you're silly enough to throw it away."

"Polly," Cecilia began slowly, "There's something else: I'm not twenty-one years old. I lied in my letter of application."

"Well, for pity's sake, girl, take that mass of dark hair you've got and twist it into a braid and stick it up on your head. Put three years on you in the blink of an eye." Polly paused, then added, "Three years *is* enough, isn't it?"

Cecilia suddenly laughed. "More than enough. I'll be twenty-one in September."

THE NEXT DAY, as Cecilia adjusted the braided twist of rich dark hair that perched on the back of her head, she wondered whether or not Polly had been right. She knew she looked older than her years, even sophisticated, but she was worried that that might not be enough to satisfy her new employer.

She splashed some cold water on her face and applied a touch of fresh lipstick. Despite the long hours spent on the train, the creamy radiance of her skin glowed with good health. The soft rounded features of her heart-shaped face contrasted with her dark hair and thick feathery eyelashes, giving her an exotic look that she had never felt quite suited her.

She straightened up in the small train rest room, feeling a slight cramp in the small of her back. At five feet nine inches tall, she was used to bending to see herself in mirrors, but the task was far more difficult on a moving train. Taking one last look in the mirror, she suddenly realized that the train was beginning to slow down. It had to be entering Dartmouth Station, she thought anxiously.

Cecilia hurried back down the aisle and began to wrestle her suitcase out of the luggage rack. There was no turning back now, she decided.

Maybe the Honorable Evan Cedric-Browne had behaved perfectly normally for an English aristocrat, if somewhat imperiously. And if he turned out to be a monster, well, nothing could stop her from taking the next train back to London. Not that she had any reason to believe she'd soon find another job if she returned. . . .

With a jolt the train came to a stop. Cecilia gathered her things, smoothed her skirt and quickly adjusted the kelly-green silk scarf tied loosely around her neck. Then she hefted her old leather suitcase and drew a deep breath. Nervously she stepped out onto the platform, repeating to herself, "Rather tall, dark-haired, tan trench coat, large cordovan case. . . ."

Cecilia gasped as she scanned the crowd. Only one man on the platform could be Evan Cedric-Browne, and she found herself staring at him in unabashed awe.

Evan Cedric-Browne seemed to her to be a giant. The man who was now striding toward her was surely six-feet-five, perhaps more. Broad shoulders topped his

large frame, and his stiff carriage gave him an almost
forbidding appearance. His hair was of a dark brown
color, streaked with gray, and it blew slightly in the
night breeze. His trench coat hung open, and Cecilia
noticed that he carried a large cordovan case, unmistakably an art portfolio.

"I see you got my letter, Miss Bennett," he said confidently, reaching for her suitcase. "My car is near the
front of the parking lot, through the station."

Cecilia suddenly found herself unable to move. She
was waiting for a proper introduction to follow, but
Evan was already walking down the platform. With a
start she hurried after him, wondering how he could be
so sure she was indeed the new tour guide at Chesterton
Manor.

"I'm Cecilia Bennett," she said as she caught up with
him. "I'm very pleased to meet you, Mr. Cedric-
Browne...sir."

Evan raised a bushy brown-and-gray eyebrow and
cast her a look that made her feel decidedly uncomfort-
able. The faint shadow of a smile crossed his face. "'Sir'
is overdoing it a bit, Miss Bennett. This is not a job
interview, and Mr. Cedric-Browne is adequately defer-
ential all by itself." After a moment he added, "Why
don't you call me Evan? After all, I'm *not* old enough to
be your father."

"I didn't think that you were. I mean, I...please call
me Cecilia," she stammered.

Cecilia looked at him closely as they entered the well-
lit station. She guessed that he was only in his early thir-
ties, but she was shocked to see that he looked as if he
hadn't slept in days. The lines of fatigue that clustered

around his eyes made her wonder if his strange attitude was the result of exhaustion. Though his movements were quick and assured, she suspected he was probably functioning on pure adrenaline.

"You look very tired," Cecilia said easily. "Would you like me to carry my own bag?"

Again Evan shot her a peculiar look, and Cecilia supposed she had said the wrong thing. Suddenly she felt as confused as she had a few weeks before, when she'd stepped into the bright lights of the terminal at Heathrow Airport. It was all so different from Africa.... But she had been proud of how gracefully she had handled herself in all her failed job interviews. It hadn't been easy; London was a long way from Kenya....

So why should all her poise desert her now, she asked herself uneasily. Vowing to be more reserved, Cecilia kept silent as they made their way through the station and into the parking lot. Evan stopped behind an old black Morris Minor in the first row of cars, and even in the dim light of the parking lot Cecilia could see that it was badly scraped and dented. It didn't seem possible that this old wreck could be owned by the same man who used sealing wax and fine stationery, she thought in surprise. Puzzled, she walked around to the passenger door after Evan had stowed her suitcase in the trunk. He opened the passenger door with a key, then held the door for her.

"I don't care to have anyone rifling through my car," he explained. "It's always locked."

Cecilia wasn't sure what he really meant. Was he saying that it was customary to keep one's car open or locked in a town of this size? Maybe he sealed his letters with wax because he thought someone might rifle through his correspondence, too.

"Oh, I understand," she said casually, hoping that sooner or later she'd come to understand English customs.

But Evan only shook his head, and Cecilia resigned herself to the fact that she and her new employer hadn't hit it off well. Suddenly, as the engine rumbled into life, her feeling of resignation disappeared. All the confusion she had been experiencing twisted together to form a tight knot of fear in her stomach. What was she thinking of, to be driving off into the night with a complete stranger? She no longer cared how aristocrats behaved in England. She refused to be treated with less than common courtesy.

"Wait!" she shouted. "I demand to know what's going on!"

Evan rubbed the bridge of his nose wearily and turned in his seat to face her. Cecilia was instantly reassured by the calm rich resonance of his voice when he spoke. "'What's going on,' Cecilia, is that we are beginning a thirty-minute drive to Chesterton Manor, where I live and where you shall soon live and work as a tour guide. It's now roughly twenty minutes to eleven. I am, as you so perceptively observed, very tired. I would suspect that five hours on a train has left you eager for a good night's sleep, too. It seems logical to me that we should discuss the details of our association once we're on our way."

The glow from the dashboard was reflected in Evan's smoky green eyes, and Cecilia thought the eyes were pleading with her not to add to the unnamed pressures that weighed on him. She was no longer afraid, and she willed herself to be patient.

"All right," she said at last in a quiet voice.

Within moments the car had passed out of the town and they turned onto an unlit country road. The crescent moon hidden behind the clouds provided almost no light, and the headlights of the car cut a path through the blackness. For several minutes Cecilia toyed absently with her silk scarf. She was waiting for Evan to begin the conversation that would answer the question that had been buzzing through her head for the past twenty-four hours.

But when she glanced over at him she realized that he seemed to have forgotten all about her. His brow was wrinkled in deep concentration, and his hands gripped the steering wheel. She couldn't begin to imagine what was troubling him, but she knew what was troubling her. She had to have some answers, and it was clear that the only way she was going to get them was by starting the conversation herself.

"You say you live at Chesterton Manor," she began in the most casual tone she could manage. "Is it a family estate?"

Evan seemed startled to hear her voice. "No," he said quietly, "it's not."

"Then who owns the manor?" Cecilia tried again. "For example, who will be paying my salary as tour guide? I assume I will receive a salary," she added, unable to keep a touch of sarcasm out of her voice.

"Yes, you will," came the terse reply. "Paid by the eleventh earl of Chesterton."

"Who's the—" Cecilia began, but the next words caught in her throat. This was silly, she thought. She wasn't going to learn much if this man wasn't willing to offer simple information voluntarily. She heaved a sigh of frustration and cast another quick glance at the strange man behind the wheel. As far as she was concerned, there was no point in going ahead with the job if this was the level of communication she could expect.

Evan's voice broke into her thoughts. "Is something troubling you?" he asked, not taking his eyes off the narrow road.

"Yes!" Cecilia blurted out. "How am I supposed to feel enthusiastic about a job when my employer won't tell me basic facts about the job or the place where I'll be working? All things, I might add, that should have been discussed in a proper interview." Cecilia paused for a breath, but her anger and frustration forced her to continue. "Don't you think you're behaving rather rudely?"

Evan laughed shortly, and for a moment Cecilia thought she saw him relax. He reached into the breast pocket of his green glen-plaid suit jacket and extracted a pack of cigarettes. Wordlessly he lighted a cigarette.

"You're right, of course," he said easily. "I'm sorry. I've got a great deal on my mind right now. I'm afraid I'm preoccupied with...other concerns. The tours at the manor are my responsibility, but I've had virtually no time to give to the project." He paused, then concluded, "You might have noted that the end of June is a bit late to be arranging to provide tours. The tourist season is well under way."

Cecilia smiled tightly. "I feel honored at this explanation," she said evenly.

Evan returned her smile briefly, but he kept his eyes riveted to the road. "The job can easily be described for now," he began. "You will lead tours through the historic wing of Chesterton Manor. I'll take you around tomorrow and give you all the details, but basically you will work a seven-hour day, six days a week. The crowds can get quite heavy at the height of the season, and I'm sure you'll find them challenging—in contrast to the boredom you are certain to feel at telling the same tales and describing the same things hour after hour. However, you'll find the money good, particularly if you figure in the generous tips you're sure to receive.

"You'll have your own suite on the ground floor of the historic—or east—wing, but you'll take your midday and evening meals with the family in the main dining room. That's in the west wing of the house—or castle, as the tourists seems to prefer."

Cecilia breathed a sigh of relief. No garret, no leftovers—and hard work didn't scare her.

"Now, as for the family," Evan went on, "my older brother, Philip, is the eleventh earl of Chesterton—the man who pays your salary. He owns the estate, the title and all the responsibility. His wife, Catherine, lives at the manor, too. Officially, at least," he added. "And then there's myself and my sister, Emily."

"So there are four of you?"

"Five. My brother's son, Tony, will be coming home for the summer vacation soon. Monday, as a matter of fact."

"What did you mean when you said that your sister-in-law lives at Chesterton 'officially'?" Cecilia asked, not stopping to wonder if it was a proper question.

"She prefers London."

"Oh." Cecilia had the impression that he had left something out of his answer, but she wasn't about to prod for details.

She leaned forward in her seat and peered out the windshield. As the car twisted through the countryside she was able to catch an occasional glimpse of the roadside area, and she noted that they were now traveling through a hilly forested area. In the extreme darkness she had the feeling that she and this odd man were the only people in the world. But the idea didn't frighten her. She felt perfectly safe with Evan Cedric-Browne now. And she wanted to know more about him.

"Wasn't that an art portfolio you were carrying at the station?" she asked in a friendly tone.

But the answer never came. Suddenly the sound of a shot pierced the silence of the night. Alarmed, Cecilia cried out. Another shot rang out, this time much closer. Evan abruptly switched off the headlights of the car.

"Get down!" he ordered.

Cecilia crouched down in the car, resting her head behind the gearshift. Involuntarily she reached for Evan's coat and found herself clutching it in fear.

The car accelerated. Evan drove faster and faster in the pitch-darkness of the winding roadway.

"Probably a hunter," Evan explained, but the tone of his voice clearly suggested he didn't believe it.

Cecilia didn't believe it, either. She had heard plenty of shots fired in her days in Africa. And she knew men did not respond to them by behaving as if they were being pursued—unless they were. Someone was trying to kill Evan Cedric-Browne. Now her own life was in danger, she thought, terrified.

Another shot rang out. Cecilia's heart pounded. There had to be two pursuers. The car was traveling too rapidly for the first marksman still to be firing from such close range. The tires shrieked as they rounded a bend and another shot exploded. The windshield shattered and the little Morris Minor swerved dangerously.

Cecilia was thrown against Evan's side, and she felt a massive hand squeeze her shoulder briefly. The pressure gave her courage, and she clung unashamedly to Evan's powerful body as he expertly guided the car around unseen curves, driving blindly with no lights and a shattered windshield.

Abruptly the shots ceased. The minutes ticked by, but still Cecilia clutched at Evan, and still the car rushed forward at a treacherous pace.

At last Cecilia felt Evan ease up on the accelerator. The car seemed to be rumbling over a wooden bridge. A comforting arm now encircled her, and Cecilia leaned into the awkward embrace.

"We're home now," Evan said quietly.

THE KINDLING CRACKLED loudly, and flames began to lick up over the single log that had been placed in the grate. The fire cast a warm circle of light around the small white stone fireplace. Cecilia eased back into the comfortable chair before the fire and felt her shivering subside as she stared into the flames.

"You didn't have to light a fire," she said, turning to Evan. "It seems silly in late June."

"You needed one," Evan said simply. "These old

stone-and-brick mansions can give you a chill when you're not used to them."

Cecilia's deep brown eyes flashed her consternation at the weary man standing just a few feet from her. She was not shivering because of the cold, and he knew it.

"I want to know—" she began.

"It must have been a foolish hunter...a poacher afraid of being caught. He was firing blindly in the night. It happens sometimes in the off-season...." Evan's voice trailed off.

"You know that's a lie," Cecilia insisted. "Someone was—"

"Let's make it true, then," Evan cut in. "Our truth and our secret." His hands, slightly trembling, rested on the back of a delicate yellow chintz armchair while his troubled eyes expressed the "please" he could not speak.

"I'm not in the habit of lying," Cecilia said angrily. "I might have been killed!" She was infuriated to think that she would be denied an explanation.

"You *never* lie?" Evan asked casually. "Not even perhaps about your age?"

Cecilia's eyes widened. "How did you know?" she said in surprise.

"You just told me," he replied with a bemused smile. "Besides, the 'hunter's' carelessness and our, uh, exciting drive has caused your hair to fall down. With the single braid trailing down your back you look, well, your age. And beautiful," he added gently.

"Lying about my age—by only a few months—is hardly comparable to pretending that that nightmare drive was...was nothing!" Cecilia retorted. She had not missed his compliment. And perversely she knew that it pleased her, yet she couldn't bring herself to let him know the impact he'd had on her.

"No, the lies aren't really equal in weight," he conceded.

"How can you be so calm?" Cecilia demanded, rising from her chair and walking toward him so that they were now only inches apart. "How dare you behave so casually when something terrible, something you obviously understand, has put *my* life—"

Evan raised his arms and cupped her elbows with his hands. The power of his touch instantly silenced her.

"Trust me, Cecilia," he said. "Believe me when I tell you that this...this has nothing to do with you, that you're perfectly safe now. It was an accident, that's all." His hands fell away, and he moved toward the door.

Cecilia desperately searched for something to say, for the words that would keep him from turning the door handle on which his hand now rested. How could he leave without telling her why they'd both been nearly killed?

"Why did you pick me—from all the applications you must have received—without even meeting me first?" she blurted out.

"Because I knew you would be on that train," he answered. "I know London. And I know that young women who have spent their lives on game preserves in Kenya are not exactly in high demand at the moment, no matter how richly and profoundly they have educated themselves under the shade of the acacia trees. As I told you in the car, I didn't have time to waste trying to settle this matter of the tours."

Cecilia was stung by his reply. So, he *did* know that

she had taken the job in desperation, that she wouldn't turn it down—because she couldn't. And he had treated her cavalierly, knowing that she was without options.

"You must have a difficult time engaging tour guides then," she shot back. "It strikes me as rather odd that there wouldn't be plenty of eager applicants right in Dartmouth—if there weren't some rumor, some stigma attached to Chesterton Manor!"

"You're quite right," Evan replied, turning the handle of the door. "Do sleep well. I'll call for you tomorrow morning."

Chapter 2

The sound was so faint that at first Cecilia could not discern what it was. She tossed in the unfamiliar bed, thinking she must still be dreaming. When the sound persisted she realized she was not dreaming.

Propping herself up on her elbows, she blinked at the strange bedroom. "Chesterton Manor," she said aloud. The words made the terrifying gunshots of last night pound in her head, and she dove back under the sheets, not wanting to think about what had happened.

But what was that sound? She sat up in bed and strained her ears. Music...someone was playing the piano very softly, almost sadly.

She reached over to her night table and turned the watch face toward her. Seven-fifteen! *Who could possibly be awake at this hour*, Cecilia wondered.

She bounded out of bed and instantly felt lightheaded. The room was stiflingly hot—and oddly dark for this hour. She hurried to open the bedroom window

and was greeted by waves of steamy air. The picture
outside her window explained the somber light: heavy
black clouds hung low in the sky, promising a stormy
summer day.

The melancholy strains of the piano were quite clear
now, and Cecilia recognized the piece as one of
Tchaikovsky's concertos, but she could not remember
which one. She glanced out again at the clouds and
thought how appropriate the music was to the day. The
pianist was not only very accomplished, but also
seemed to possess a perverse sense of mood.

Finding it vaguely disturbing to have so little sense of
her surroundings, Cecilia walked barefoot out of the
bedroom and into the private adjoining sitting room.
The room had been luxuriously furnished with a
woman's tastes in mind. Various shades of white and
yellow were complemented by the pale tones of blond
oak in the furniture, and one wall was entirely covered
by a built-in oak bookcase. A quick glance of the books
told Cecilia that the subjects were related primarily to
the history of England and Devonshire. A few large
volumes on a lower shelf were devoted to the history of
the Cedric-Browne family and Chesterton Manor,
books that she looked forward to exploring.

But first she wanted to gain a sense of perspective.
She and Evan had entered the manor from the back the
previous night and had walked down one short corridor
to the door of her suite. That was all she knew. Except
that she was on the ground floor, in the east wing. And
that the thought of Evan made her feel strangely dizzy
when combined with the oppressive atmosphere of the
closed room.

Pulling aside the heavy velvet draperies drawn across the window, she saw that the room faced the front courtyard of the manor. Then, craning her neck to see to her left, she made out the beginnings of a formal garden bordered by an ancient boxwood hedge. Straight ahead was the bridge she and Evan had crossed late last night.

Again the memory of that awful drive assaulted her thoughts. The last thing she recalled was glancing back at Evan's car, parked behind the manor, its windshield totally shattered.

Her thoughts instantly drew her eyes back to the bridge, and for the first time she saw why a bridge was necessary. The manor appeared to be surrounded by a very wide moat. Under the menacing skies, the water had a hard stone-gray color, and in the muggy stillness of the day its dull surface was strangely flat.

Cecilia let the draperies fall together, closing out the grudging light that had crept into the room. The music was beginning to depress her. The pianist had started the piece over again, though why, Cecilia could not imagine. The recital was utterly flawless, and the repetition was unnerving. It was as if the pianist were insisting that all those who could hear assume the deep sorrow of the melody.

The volume of the music increased slightly as Cecilia made her way back into the bedroom. She assumed the piano must be above her bed—and that the pianist must have known that playing would awaken her. That rudeness, Cecilia decided, would be characteristic of Evan, judging from his behavior on the previous evening. Was he playing the piano, or was some other member of the

Cedric-Browne family equally inconsiderate? It was not a possibility that she was eager to contemplate.

Looking out the bedroom window of her suite, Cecilia saw that it had the distinction of facing a small parking lot just big enough for about four cars. Three cars now occupied the space, Evan's Morris Minor being the closest one to her window.

Evan's car! Cecilia was astonished as she looked at it. The windshield appeared to be brand-new. There wasn't a crack or a scratch on it. But she knew for a fact that just a few hours ago the glass had been shattered out in every corner.

The pianist suddenly stopped in the middle of a musical phrase, then began the piece again.

Cecilia felt slightly unbalanced. She was by nature an optimistic person, and yet nearly every moment since she had stepped off the train in Dartmouth had been filled with confusion and fear. Well, she told herself spiritedly, she would have to put an end to that. Never mind when Evan was planning to call for her. She would bathe and dress and do some exploring on her own. After all, he had said that this was to be her house—castle—too.

CECILIA STOOD HESITANTLY in the hallway just outside the door to her sitting room, wondering where and how she should begin her expedition. She had twisted her hair back up on top of her head and chosen a simple green-and-white cotton dress to combat the heaviness of the day. But now she could feel a growing stickiness just under the narrow white belt that accentuated her slender waist, and she longed for the relief of some cool air.

Before she could decide which way to turn she heard a strange offbeat shuffling noise. The irregular beat was punctuated by a heavy sound, as if something were striking the highly polished parquet floor. The sound was coming closer. Someone was limping toward her.

"Do you always wander around in other people's homes?" an accusing voice suddenly demanded.

Cecilia was stunned by the appearance of the speaker. She wore a floor-length beige bathrobe of a dowdy style, and a pair of battered-looking bedroom slippers. A tangle of unruly brown hair surrounded her face, a face that was alive with both intelligence and menace. The woman, who appeared to be in her late twenties, bore an unmistakable resemblance to Evan Cedric-Browne, and Cecilia wondered whether this was his sister, Emily.

"I live here now," Cecilia began, gesturing vaguely at the closed door to her suite. "I arrived last—"

"I know who you are," the woman interrupted. "As you may have guessed, I, too, live here." She tugged at the side of her bathrobe.

"I see," Cecilia said haltingly. "You must be Emily Cedric-Browne."

"How perceptive of you," the woman remarked.

Cecilia was becoming flustered by such unprovoked hostility. "I'm sorry if I startled you," she tried again, "but I've been awake for a while, and I thought I might just take some time to familiarize myself with—"

"Evan will familiarize you with everything you *need* to know," Emily said sternly. "Until such time, I suggest that you go back to your rooms and exercise a little good taste by not prowling about unannounced."

Cecilia's brown eyes widened in disbelief. A retort sprang to her lips, but the harsh young woman was in full control.

"Gwen will be around shortly with your breakfast. I shouldn't think you'll have to languish for Evan much longer after that." Not waiting for a reply, Emily turned on her heel and continued down the hall.

Cecilia didn't know what to do. It was against her grain to let herself be bullied. Still, Evan had not expressly said that she was free to come and go as she pleased. She wavered momentarily in the hall, then decided to play it safe on her first morning. She would discuss the matter with Evan as soon as she saw him.

As she slipped back into her room Cecilia had a sudden and unaccountable wish that she had locked her door. Although people within a household often don't lock their bedroom doors, at that moment Cecilia definitely did not feel as if she were a part of a household. She felt like an unwelcome intruder. And there were items among her belongings that she did not want disturbed.

She stared at her open suitcase. The logical way to occupy her time would be to unpack, but the idea did not appeal to her. As long as her possessions were in that suitcase, she could remain undecided. The ominous admission that Evan had made last night about Chesterton carrying a stigma had not yet been explained to her. But her meeting with Emily, his sister, gave her some ideas as to what that stigma might be.

Abruptly, Cecilia strode over and slammed shut the huge old suitcase. Its scarred leather surface reminded her of warm meaningful moments long ago. The case had been the one she and her father had shared on her only trip to London. She knew that she had been born in London, but that the first six months of her life had been spent in the great city now held no meaning for her. No...instead she remembered the reasons for the trip she and her father had taken....

She was only nine years old when the report had come that her frail mother had been mauled to death by a lioness. Everyone accepted the fact that the lions were a serious threat during the dry season. Little Cecilia was warned of the danger each day. But understandably, she had not been able to accept her own mother's death. She was inconsolable.

Her father had acted decisively. He had taken the still crying little girl directly from the funeral to the airport and on to London, where he devoted himself entirely to his anguished daughter. And in time, Cecilia came to laugh again. Only when she had begged to return to Africa did they fly back to the modest residence of the game warden of the largest preserve in Kenya. It was the only home Cecilia had ever known, and with her father's love to sustain her, she was prepared to accept its dangers.

It hardly seemed possible that her father was gone now, too, Cecilia mused. She had stayed on in Kenya for a few weeks after his quiet painless death, but she had known that it was no place for her. The country had changed. Her father had been among the last of the respected colonials, and he had been beseeched to stay long after most of the others had left. But for Cecilia there was no future on the turbulent continent of Africa. And now all that remained of those happy years was the suitcase, her memories and her inheritance.

She ran her fingers absently back and forth over a tiny rip in the side of the case and felt the tears begin to form in her eyes. If only she had someone to talk to.... Even Polly had been important to her, she now realized. She had never felt alone, knowing Polly was just a few steps from her hotel.... Her eyes fell on the ornate French telephone on her writing table, but there was no one she wanted to call, no one she cared to turn to. A few tears broke forth, but Cecilia resolutely brushed them away. Someone was knocking at the door, and she hastily composed herself.

"Come in," she called, her voice sounding unnaturally loud to her.

"Good mornin'," cried the young girl who hurried immediately into the sitting room. She set a large tray on the round table by the fireplace, then straightened up and appraised Cecilia critically. "I'm Gwen," she said, smiling. "You must be the latest addition to this happy manor."

Cecilia smiled instantly in return. It was the first time that anyone connected with Chesterton Manor had taken the trouble to initiate a proper introduction. The experience was refreshing. "Hello, I'm Cecilia Bennett, the new tour guide."

"All the tour guides are new, Miss Bennett," Gwen replied casually. "Never any guide gets 'old' around here. And I don't fancy myself getting old in this here monster of a place, either." Gwen gestured to the pots on the tray. "Tea or coffee?" she asked. "Didn't know what to bring, so I figured I'd bring both, this bein' your first mornin' and all."

"Tea, please," answered Cecilia. She smiled again as Gwen handed her the fragile china cup.

"Now, there's toast," Gwen began, indicating the tray once more, "and a heap of perfect Devon butter as well as some marmalade."

"It all looks very nice," Cecilia commented. "Do you come every day, Gwen?"

"I live here, Miss Bennett, and you'd better believe they keep me busy—seven days a week."

"Seven days a week!" Cecilia exclaimed.

"I'm the only one—the only maid, that is. When the rest of the staff cleared out, I jumped at the chance to take over. And I don't complain. I didn't have a choice, you see," she concluded brightly.

"No, I don't really see," Cecilia replied wonderingly. It was unthinkable to her that only one girl, and as spare as Gwen, could be the sole domestic in a mansion the size of Chesterton. She sat down on the delicate bentwood chair by the writing table and studied Gwen. "The whole staff left at once?" she probed.

"The whole lot of 'em—twelve. And real professionals, too. Why, some of 'em were even born here at Chesterton." Gwen busied herself by shifting the items on the oval breakfast tray so that the sterling-silver toast rack was clearly visible to Cecilia.

"Do you know why?"

"No," replied Gwen, straightening up. "Oh, there's lots of rumors about, mind you. Some folks say the Cedric-Brownes are clean out of money. But there's more to it than that. I had my eyes open walkin' in here."

"And yet you took the job," Cecilia said, placing her

empty cup on the leather-topped writing table and crossing her long shapely legs.

"Oh, well, 'course. Like I said, I didn't have a choice. Mum's ailing, you see, and pa died a while back, so it's up to me to look after the poor dear soul." Gwen paused to pour Cecilia a second cup of tea, placing a linen napkin under the cup so that the hot liquid wouldn't mar the smooth green leather of the desk top.

"Anyway, here at Chesterton I'm the head lady, so I work twice as hard and I get a nice pay. But if I were at some other place with lots of servants I'd probably be the lowest of the lot. Money's the thing. I wouldn't stay another day if it weren't for the opportunity here."

"But why would you leave?" Cecilia asked, intrigued. "Why does everyone leave—the staff, the tour guides?"

"Same answer to both questions, Miss Bennett," answered Gwen. She gave a touch to the white lace collar of her black uniform before saying seriously, "The place is jinxed."

Cecilia wanted to laugh, but Gwen was evidently speaking in deadly earnest. Despite all the misgivings that she herself already had about her new job at Chesterton, the notion that the estate could be "jinxed" was too simplistic for her.

"What do you mean by 'jinxed,' Gwen?" she asked, rising and walking over to help herself to a slice of toast. "And have a piece of toast," she added.

"Oh, I couldn't eat your breakfast!" Gwen exclaimed in mock horror.

"You won't be eating my breakfast, Gwen," Cecilia laughed. "And it sounds like you need to keep your strength up around here."

"Right you are," Gwen agreed, eagerly helping herself to a slice of toast and slathering it with the thick orange jam. "Haunted," she explained hastily.

"Haunted? Chesterton Manor?"

Gwen nodded vigorously, then swallowed quickly so that she could speak. "Haunted by the earl of Chesterton."

"But the earl of Chesterton is Philip Cedric—"

"The *sixth* earl of Chesterton," Gwen interrupted. She lowered her head slightly, apparently embarrassed that she had interrupted Cecilia. Although they were both technically employees, Gwen clearly felt that Cecilia was her social superior.

"The sixth earl of Chesterton," Cecilia repeated. "He must be haunting the manor from a distance of almost two centuries, Gwen," she observed.

"Sure that he does. And not just the house. The whole place is jinxed—the dairy, the stables, the orchard. And the tour guides can't take it. I'm a hardy sort, though I might not look it," Gwen said reflectively. "But," she continued more briskly, "in my time here—just over a year now—I've seen more than one young guide go dashing out in tears. Why, last summer we had seven guides in all!"

"But what does the sixth earl *do*?" Cecilia pressed.

"He haunts. Now, myself, I stay clear of him, but still I've seen plenty of odd goings-on around here. I've no reason to doubt that that old ghost is mighty mad."

Cecilia's amusement at these revelations was mixed with a certain unease. She did not share the girl's belief in ghosts, but she was receiving confirmation that something was decidedly awry at Chesterton Manor.

"Well, what's the ghost mad about?" Cecilia asked, hoping that her voice did not betray her amusement.

Gwen drew a deep breath—preparing to launch into a bloodcurdling story, Cecilia was certain—but before she exhaled, her eyes widened. "Lord, what's the time?" she suddenly asked.

Cecilia consulted her watch. "Almost nine," she replied.

"Got to be on my way. Busy around here with Master Tony coming home from school Monday, as you can imagine." The girl hurried toward the door, then paused and turned back to Cecilia. "I'll be around each morning with your breakfast at eight-thirty. And I'll collect the dishes after you've started work in the morning, if that suits you."

Cecilia nodded. It was obvious that the only person with whom she had been able to carry on a conversation was about to leave. Then she remembered something.

"Gwen," she called, stopping the girl at the door, "who was playing the piano this morning?"

"Oh, that's Lady Emily," Gwen replied. "A fine person, Lady Emily. She helps me around this big place, even does most of the cooking, she does. Nothing uppity about *that* one, at least."

Cecilia struggled to match this testimony to her own experience of the woman she had met in the hall, but something in what Gwen had said made another question come to mind. "What do you mean, 'at least'? Is there someone who's...?" She didn't know how to finish the question tactfully, but Gwen was quick to respond.

"Lady Chesterton—Catherine, Philip's wife. If ever

there was one to put on airs! Well, she's enough to make anyone want to quit this place, ghost or no ghost."

"What do you mean?"

Gwen shook her head. "I'm not a gossip, Miss Bennett. You just take my advice and watch out. This is a place where you're wise to mind your step. You don't look as if you'd be easily frightened, but until you understand. . .well, just be careful." She gave Cecilia a warm parting smile, then closed the door silently behind her.

Cecilia was sorry to see Gwen go. She'd enjoyed meeting her and was touched by the protective tone Gwen had taken as she left.

Pouring the last few drops of tea into her cup, she pondered Gwen's disclosures. What Gwen had had to say was interesting. And worrisome. Although she didn't for a minute think that Chesterton was haunted, she was indeed ready to believe that odd things happened here. Nothing about the place or her association with it so far felt comfortable.

She had been rudely treated by two Cedric-Brownes in the short time she had spent with them. Evan was a distant and peculiar man. That much was obvious, though she could not quite forget the power he had had over her, or the fascination that he had inspired in her.

His sister, Emily, on the other hand, did not inspire any fascination. Furthermore, Gwen had said that Catherine, whom Cecilia gathered was the sister-in-law Evan had mentioned, was a person to be wary of. But how much more wary could she be?

And to top it all off, the entire staff at Chesterton and a parade of tour guides before her had all fairly fled the estate. At the first sign of danger she would have to leave, Cecilia told herself firmly. Danger. Being shot at was definitely dangerous, she reflected ruefully.

A clap of thunder sliced through her thoughts. She heard the first drops of rain falling outside on the gravel drive. What had Gwen said as she'd left? That she should protect herself until she "understood." She realized that Gwen had spoken more sensibly than the young girl could have known. Cecilia, though, wasn't thinking of her physical safety at that moment. No, she had to protect her inheritance. It was the only security she had in the world now. But what was she to do with the many stacks of cash—several thousand dollars—that she had hidden in her suitcase?

She didn't feel she understood the English banking system any more now than when she had decided to leave the money in cash. Her plan had been to ask the advice of her new employer when she got a job. To her there had seemed to be so many things a person could do with a fair-sized block of money in the complicated city of London that she had chosen to wait until she was better informed.

But whose advice could she seek? She didn't feel comfortable with the notion of discussing her finances with Evan. And worse, she didn't feel comfortable knowing every penny she owned was housed at Chesterton Manor. Her inexpensive hotel in London had seemed safe. Chesterton Manor did not.

Chapter 3

The long list of questions Cecilia had resolved to ask Evan melted away a short while later. Instead she was content to gaze at him from across the short space that separated their chairs in front of her unlit fireplace. A labyrinth of fine red lines spoiled the beauty of his expressive green eyes, and she noticed the creases of weariness that were etched in his brow. Cecilia sat patiently, waiting for an explanation of what had happened the night before. Surely Evan had reconsidered the folly of dismissing an attack on their lives as "accidental," she thought to herself. Now at last he would tell her the truth.

"As I promised last night," Evan began, "I'll try to acquaint you with Chesterton and the responsibilities of being the tour guide here. You may find it a shade overwhelming at first, but I'm sure that in a week's time you'll feel quite comfortable with the position."

Cecilia was amazed at the calmness of his manner. His appearance, the events of last night and Gwen's words crashed together in her mind, and the sympathy she had felt upon first seeing him vanished.

"I gather that none of the tour guides you employed last summer ever became comfortable with the position," she challenged.

Evan did not flinch at her tone. "I don't think I attempted to deceive you on that point last night," he said evenly. "I believe you suggested that some 'stigma' was attached to the manor. That's not a word I'd be inclined to use, but it is a matter of record that the guides have not been, uh, happy."

"I think it only proper that you tell me what word you *would* use," Cecilia rejoined, folding her hands tightly in her lap.

"The situation is a complicated one and . . . ." He broke off and glanced nervously over Cecilia's shoulder, out the window. She followed his gaze but saw nothing in the front drive except the pelting rain.

"And," he continued, quickly regaining his composure, "I can only assume that a number of minor incidents have conspired to make this region rife with rumors about Chesterton." There was a slight edge to Evan's voice as he concluded, "The Cedric-Browne fortune hasn't flourished but rather has diminished in recent years. Beyond this, the family as a whole has undergone some trying times. I trust that you will have the grace not to press me further as to what they were."

"Would you consider being shot at a 'minor incident'?" she demanded.

"Cecilia, I assured you that last night had nothing to do with you or Chesterton. I beg you not to mention it ever again. The news of such a . . . well, someone who is very

dear to me would find the news extremely disturbing.
And *you* are perfectly safe."

Cecilia found herself powerless to mistrust him. She
looked down at her clasped hands, wondering who was
so special to him. Without success she tried to keep her
mind from drifting to the closeness they had shared in the
moments of danger in the car. At last she said quietly, "Is
that why you stayed up all night to replace the windshield—to hide the truth from someone you love?"

Evan stood up abruptly. With his back half turned to
her, he said softly, "Yes. In part."

Cecilia knew she had to make a decision. She could
either take this moment to announce that she was returning to London, or she could choose to stay on...and
place her trust in Evan. The thought that he loved someone with whom he could not share the hardships of his
life saddened her. And yet she had to gain some work
experience. Her inheritance eventually would be spent if
she didn't start working—and soon.

"Shall we begin the tour?" she said suddenly. "I'm
afraid that at the moment I couldn't guide anyone any
farther than to my own rooms."

For a split second Evan hesitated. Then he turned to
face her and said, "By all means."

As Cecilia closed the door to her suite behind them, he
added, quietly, "Thank you."

The tour took the better part of the morning, although
it was confined to the historic east wing of the manor.
The depth of Evan's knowledge about each piece of furniture and each memento of the Cedric-Brownes' past awed
Cecilia. He discussed the history of the manor and its
contents in minute detail, pointing out Venetian

chandeliers, fine Chippendale tables, antique crystal, brilliantly colored Persian carpets, and precious draperies embroidered with gold and silver threads.

The rooms had all been arranged to make it appear that some nameless eighteenth-century Cedric-Brownes were now occupying them. A long pecan dining table had been set for twelve with priceless Dresden china, and a high canopied bed had been made up with soft Flemish linen and turned down in mock anticipation of its owner's night's sleep. A first edition of Pope's *The Rape of the Lock* lay open in the library beside two full snifters of brandy—the setting contrived to recall the occasion on which Sir William Cavendish, then duke of Devonshire, had met in that very spot with the second earl of Chesterton.

When Cecilia protested that she would never be able to recall all there was to learn about the magnificent manor, Evan quickly reassured her. He explained that she would be given a complete written inventory of all the articles and history that pertained to the tours. In addition, the tours she would provide were to be only twenty-five minutes each in length. Whatever she could learn beyond the basic presentation would simply make her better able to answer questions.

It was nearly noon by the time Cecilia and Evan reached the upper gallery. The mansion was shaped like an H, with a long wide central hall separating the two wings. Although the east wing was technically referred to as the historic, or tourist, side, the bar of the H was actually part of the tours. Cecilia was supposed to meet the tourists on the bridge over the moat. She would then lead them through the main entrance to the castle, di-

recting them to the lower part of the H's bar. The tours
were to conclude on the upper portion of the bar, which
was the gallery.

Throughout Cecilia's private tour she had been impressed by Evan's deep pride in his family's heritage, but
when they reached the gallery she knew at once that
they'd arrived at the room that was most meaningful to
him.

"This room contains some of the finest portrait art of
the last three centuries," Evan began. "As you can see,
there are sixteen paintings in all. Most of them are
members of the Cedric-Browne family. You will want to
note especially in each of your tours these two works by
Sir Joshua Reynolds, whose influence on the art of portraiture, particularly in England, can hardly be over-
stated.

"Reynolds was, in fact, born in Devonshire, and he
began his career here in 1742. These are two of his earliest
works, commissioned while some of the work was still
being completed on Chesterton Manor itself."

Cecilia tried to listen attentively as Evan went on to
describe the facets of artistic genius represented in each of
the two paintings. Still, she couldn't help but be
distracted by the light in which he himself appeared in
this setting. He spoke as one consumed by the magic of
each brushstroke, oblivious to the fact that the increas-
ingly technical nature of his discourse would be lost on all
but the most earnest students of art.

The scene reminded her of the fact that she had never
received an answer when she had asked him about the art
portfolio he was carrying at the train station. But just as
she was about to ask him if he himself was an artist, she

realized that he was preparing to speak about another pair of paintings. Personal questions, she decided, could wait till later.

"Here are two more works that you must be certain to note in each of the tours, though not for the same reasons as you will note the Reynolds," Evan continued. He indicated two paintings that appeared to Cecilia's eyes to be less graceful than the invaluable Reynolds.

"They were done by an obscure artist named Rollings de Stangrave. You needn't mention that unless you're asked, since few people have ever heard of him."

"I must confess I haven't," Cecilia interjected, feeling that she ought to speak so that he would be sure she was still listening.

"Well, that's not important. What is important is the tale of these two characters—Reginald, the sixth earl of Chesterton, and his charming wife, Lady Eleanora."

"The sixth earl of Chesterton!" Cecilia exclaimed. "Why, he's the ghost!"

Evan let out a deep resonating laugh that filled the room. "So old Reginald has paid you a visit, has he?" he asked, still chuckling. "And how has he been throughout the centuries?"

Cecilia felt a blush spreading all the way up to her hairline. She didn't *believe* in the ghost. She was just surprised to see his portrait.

"No, he hasn't paid me a visit," she snapped, trying vainly to cover her embarrassment with anger.

"Then, obviously Gwen has," Evan surmised.

"Yes, yes. It was Gwen. A very sweet girl, I might add. Though certainly *I* don't believe in ghosts!"

"I'm sure you don't," Evan rejoined. "And did Gwen

fill you in on *why* Reginald prowls the dark corridors of his past when the moon is full?"

"Gwen didn't say anything about full moons or about the historical circumstances that have given this—this ancestor of yours a reputation such as he apparently holds."

"Well, then I must tell you, for that is the reason why you should mention these paintings. The tourists love the story of poor Reginald."

"All right, let's have it," Cecilia demanded. "It's my job to know."

"I'll be delighted to oblige. Reginald, the sixth earl of Chesterton, is, as you can see from his portrait, a number of years senior to his pretty wife, Eleanora, as well as a good foot wider. One may presume that he married her out of vanity, but in any case, he didn't live to learn what a vicious woman she was. Indeed, Eleanora was not only willing to cuckold her bloated husband, but she thought she might be best able to enjoy the wealth of Chesterton if she murdered him. And murder him she did—with strychnine. Unfortunately for Eleanora, Reginald had more friends than she had bargained for. Eleanora wasn't able to remain at Chesterton as the guardian of her young stepson, the seventh earl of Chesterton."

"What happened to her?" Cecilia asked.

"Hanged."

"Oh," was all Cecilia could manage as she stared at the gilt-framed portrait of the beautiful but treacherous Eleanora. The young woman was dressed in a scarlet gown distinguished by a shocking décolletage, and she had mountains of black hair piled on top of her head, fastened with clasps of gold that were studded with diamonds and rubies. Her glacial blue eyes seemed to stare directly at Cecilia.

"You may tell the story anyway you like during your tours," Evan went on, breaking Cecilia's concentration on the stunning woman in the painting, "but I have observed that the tourists are most happy when you play it for all the dramatics that the tale offers."

"Certainly," Cecilia replied, hoping that she sounded businesslike. "I can well imagine that what you say is true."

Evan cast her a bemused look and walked over to one of the long waist-high glass cases that occupied the center of the gallery.

"Here," he said, "is the best way to conclude your recital of this chilling moment in the tragic history of the Cedric-Brownes." He indicated a small tightly corked glass vial in the case. With horror, Cecilia read the age-yellowed label. The white powder in the vial was strychnine.

"Is this . . . the poison that . . ." she stammered.

"The very bottle and what is left of the instrument of the dastardly deed," Evan confirmed, smiling.

Cecilia spun on the balls of her feet to face him. Her brown eyes flashed with anger. "Why do you find this so funny?" she demanded. "One of your ancestors was hideously murdered in this very house. And you keep the . . . the murder weapon as a grisly memento and," she concluded, "a dependable lure for the tourist dollar!"

Evan's hearty laugh filled the room again. "No, I don't find it amusing—most of the time. But," he said with a disarming grin, "I couldn't resist playing on your spellbound attraction to the portrait. I must remember to thank Gwen for setting things up so nicely."

For a moment the only sound in the room was that of the rain beating against the floor-to-ceiling-paneled windows of beveled glass that ran the length of the south wall of the room. Cecilia glared at Evan, but she couldn't bring herself to begrudge him a moment of amusement— even if it was at her expense.

Finally she broke into a warm smile. "That's quite a story, Mr. Cedric-Browne, sir."

"Evan," he smiled in return. "Do call me Evan."

Cecilia nodded, feeling a sudden and inexplicable shyness sweep over her. She stood motionless in confused silence for what seemed an eternity. Then the moment was lost when she saw Evan glance at his watch.

"I have several calls that I must make before luncheon," he said, "so I hope you'll excuse me. We all generally assemble in the dining room at one o'clock; until that time you're free to wander about the wing as you like. This rain makes a tour of the grounds impossible, and you'll meet the family soon enough."

"I've already met your sister," Cecilia began. Instantly she saw Evan's face cloud. "This morning.... She seemed to be unhappy to find me in the hall and—"

"Emily has a rather fragile personality," Evan interrupted. "I would suggest that you give her a wide berth until you and she have had an opportunity to become better acquainted."

He left Cecilia no room to continue the conversation, but concluded harshly, "You should have no trouble finding your way to the dining room. Just proceed along the main hall on the lower floor until you come to the end. Then make a right turn. You'll find yourself in the salon. The dining room is adjoining."

"Of course," Cecilia replied curtly. "You needn't draw me a map."

THE WALK down the vast hall joining the two wings of Chesterton Manor seemed to be one of the longest in Cecilia's life. The morning had been a seesaw of emotions for her, and approaching this introductory luncheon with the Cedric-Browne family was not something she looked forward to.

When she reached the salon, now empty, she paused a moment to absorb its discordant appearance. Like all the other rooms she had seen in the manor, the salon was made grand by its very spaciousness. Yet Cecilia was sure that if she raised her voice it would echo. Although each piece of furniture was indisputably elegant and valuable, she had the fleeting impression that the family's living quarters had been raided to create the luxurious settings in the east wing—the income-generating space in the manor.

Evan's voice cut through her speculation. Cecilia realized instantly that he must be in the dining room. He seemed to be having an argument with some other family member.

"You will not go to London, Catherine," she heard him shout. "And I see no room for further discussion. Two of your shopping sprees in one month are quite enough."

"I hardly see that it's any of your business," a woman's voice rejoined angrily.

"Chesterton is my business," came Evan's reply. "And how we're going to pay for the repairs to the barn roof is everyone's concern! On a day like today the rain pours through onto the animals and—"

Cecilia could tell that someone had interrupted Evan, but she couldn't make out the words. Should she break in on their argument? Or worse, stand here eavesdropping?

"Exactly." It was Evan speaking again. "It's impossible for you to leave with Tony coming the day after tomorrow."

Philip's son, Cecilia thought. She checked her watch and saw that it was five past one. The conversation didn't sound as if it were ending, but sooner or later she would have to make an appearance.

The entrance to the dining room was at the other end of the salon. Noiselessly Cecilia crossed to the door and stood hesitantly on the threshold, waiting to be invited in. For several seconds no one noticed her. Then Emily spoke.

"Ah, the new tour guide," she said unpleasantly. "Are you an expert at eavesdropping, or is it a new experience for you?"

"I wasn't. . .I just. . . ." Cecilia gestured toward the salon, hoping to indicate that she had just arrived.

"Come in, Cecilia," interjected Evan. "Let me introduce you to the family."

Cecilia stepped gingerly into the room and saw that the foursome was grouped around a silver tray of iced drinks set on the buffet at the end of the room. She was mildly surprised to see the transformation that had taken place in Emily since their meeting in the hall. The woman was now neatly dressed, although not fashionably. Still, it was easy to see that she could be very attractive if she took more interest in her appearance.

Catherine and Philip were a study in contrasts. That they could be married simply amazed Cecilia. Philip was tall, like his brother, but plump and fleshy about the face. He was dressed entirely in khaki, and his knees were soiled with grass stains.

Catherine, on the other hand, was a ravishing beauty. Waves of golden hair cascaded around her striking features, and the sheath of white silk that she wore sensuously caressed the curves of her shapely figure. Cecilia had a strange feeling that she had seen Catherine before but dismissed the idea as impossible.

"This is my brother, Philip," Evan began, "the eleventh earl of Chesterton."

An unassuming smile crossed Philip's puffy face, and he stretched out his hand. "Pleased to meet you, Cecilia. And forget that I'm a lord. I usually do." Cecilia could easily see how Evan had had the temerity to rebuke this man's wife. The earl looked utterly helpless.

"I'm very pleased to meet you," Cecilia started to say, but Evan pushed ahead with the introductions.

"And this is Catherine—or Lady Chesterton, if she prefers," Evan added sarcastically.

Catherine paid no attention to the remark. She smiled broadly at Cecilia, saying, "I'm so pleased to meet you, Cecilia. Your stunning height will be a tremendous advantage to you in talking over the crowds this summer." Then she added in an even more friendly voice, "But I hope you won't let Evan work you too hard. The ventilation in some of these old rooms is not the best on a hot day. You must have noticed that this morning."

Cecilia smiled. "Yes, it is a bit warm—"

"And Emily I believe you've met," Evan continued, talking over Cecilia.

Emily managed to nod and glare at the same time, but said nothing. At that moment Gwen entered with a large platter of cold meats. Emily turned immediately to help the girl place the platter on the table, and Evan motioned them all toward the table. While Cecilia was taking her seat next to Catherine, she watched in silence as Gwen and Emily carried in a colorful array of cold salads. The group began to pass the various dishes around the table, and Cecilia soon began to feel nervous once more. The family obviously considered her an intruder.

She had expected to be asked questions on this her first meal with the family, giving everyone a chance to get acquainted. But she ate in silence as the rest of the family engaged in a sparing discussion of topics upon which she could not possibly comment. She reflected that Emily, Gwen and Evan had each suggested that she somehow make herself invisible. It proved to be an easy task.

Toward the end of the meal the conversation became especially heated, and Cecilia fought to think of a graceful way to excuse herself. But the argument continued without break.

"I simply can't understand how you can contemplate going through another summer with that monster. With Tony coming home Monday, I have to feel that you're flirting with disaster," Catherine was insisting.

"Tchaikovsky is mine," Emily said angrily. "And I resent your calling him a monster, Catherine."

"Well, he is! You should know that better than anyone else," Catherine retorted. "He's eating us out of house and home! All this talk about money, and we keep—"

"That's enough, Catherine," Evan commanded. "I pay Tchaikovsky's bills. His upkeep does not come out of the household accounts. Unlike your upkeep, which—"

"Evan! How dare you! I am not a horse," Catherine snapped.

"And Tchaikovsky is not *your* horse," Emily interrupted.

"Emily," Catherine began soothingly, "I know how you love the animal, but you've really got to learn to exercise some judgment. Now, we're all trying to do our part to maintain Chesterton, and if you would only consent to sell the beast, then the barn roof—"

"The two are not related, Catherine, and you know it," Emily shouted.

Evan rose. "I think we've all had enough lunch," he said. "The discussion is closed." Cecilia reddened as she felt his eyes turning to her for the first time during the meal. "Would you care for anything more from the kitchen, Cecilia?"

Cecilia was on her feet in a flash. "No," she answered, trying to restrain her anger at the way the entire family had behaved. "I've had quite enough, thank you." And with that she left the room, wondering how she would ever find the tolerance required to remain at Chesterton Manor.

Chapter 4

The bright summer sun brought out the beauty of the landscape to perfection, Cecilia thought as she retraced the country road she and Evan had taken from Dartmouth three nights before. Great rolling hills of stunning emerald green were dotted with fat sheep and velvety Jersey cows. Isolated fruit trees whose branches spread out into perfect round tops, and feathery hedges punctuated the bends and curves of the land. Here and there the steeple of a pristine white church poked through the foliage, and a patch of red brick homes—the nexus of some small village—would come into view. In the wooded areas small thatched cottages were visible from the road, giving the drive a timeless flavor.

Cecilia was almost disappointed to see Dartmouth ahead, but the quaint town proved to be as charming as the countryside that surrounded it. She guided the car carefully down the narrow cobbled streets that led

to the waterfront, feeling freer and happier than she had
since she'd left Kenya.

Sunday had been just as rainy as Saturday, and she
had spent a gloomy day in the east wing rehearsing her
tour speech. But this morning had dawned clear and
beautiful, and she'd had an amazing encounter with the
stern Emily.

She had been instantly on guard when she entered the
conservatory and found Emily preparing to practice.
However, Emily had surprised her by smiling and sug-
gesting that after two days of stormy weather Cecilia
might enjoy an excursion to Dartmouth. She had given
Cecilia excellent directions and permission to use her car,
explaining that she did not give piano lessons on Mon-
days. Her kindness had seemed genuine, and Cecilia was
inclined to believe that the woman sometimes used
hostile tactics to cover a basic sense of insecurity.
Perhaps Emily was becoming used to her, she thought
hopefully, and in time they could become friends.

Cecilia knew that luck was with her when she spotted a
convenient parking place right near the water. She
parked and then decided to take a stroll through the ship-
yards of this tiny port on the Dart river's estuary. She
knew that the shipbuilding industry had been established
in Dartmouth for centuries, and as she watched the men
at work she had the impression that fine craftsmanship
was still highly valued here.

When Cecilia reached the splendid yachting center that
Emily had told her about she was pleased to discover a
pleasant-looking pub named Edward III on the water's
edge. A number of tables had been placed on the patio,
and she decided to enjoy an early lunch.

Inside she bought a newspaper and a plowman's lunch of sharp white English cheddar, brown bread, Devonshire butter, chutney and pickled onions. Though it was Monday, she felt herself in a holiday mood and decided to indulge in a half-pint of lager.

Neither the meal nor the setting was a disappointment, but Cecilia's lunch was dominated by a front-page story in the local newspaper. She was shocked to read that the area around Dartmouth was experiencing a crime wave, particularly thefts of art treasures. It was hard for her to believe that this lovely region could be harboring any criminals. She was also amazed to read of the number of wealthy landholders with elegant estates so close by. She had wrongly assumed that Chesterton Manor was unique in an area of largely agricultural focus. Instead, as she read the story in the paper, she learned that titled families from London had flocked to Devonshire, building summer homes and mansions with furnishings to match their regal incomes.

With regret Cecilia realized that she ought to be getting back to Chesterton. She would have loved to take a guidebook in hand and spend the entire day wandering around Dartmouth. But she knew that she had to get back so that she would have time to practice her speech. The next day she would be giving her first tours.

The drive back to Chesterton was just as lovely as the drive into Dartmouth had been, but Cecilia's mind kept returning to the newspaper article...and the vulnerability of Chesterton. A thief, she realized, could spend days looting the many treasures at the manor. Surely there must be an elaborate security system? Yet she had never observed anything to indicate that there was one.

Evan had given her a set of keys that opened the glass cases in the upper gallery, and the strongbox where she was to keep each day's tour money before turning it all over to him at the end of each week. He had cautioned her that the velvet ropes separating the contents of the rooms from the tourists were not foolproof and that she should be on guard for any "enterprising" visitor who might reach across the rope and pinch a small prize.

As she slowed the car to cross the narrow wooden bridge over the Chesterton moat she determined that the first thing that she would do would be to find Evan. She parked in the back, noting that Evan's car was gone, then entered through the rear entrance of the east wing. Quickly depositing her purse in her sitting room, Cecilia headed down the central hall in search of Evan, reasoning that someone else might have borrowed his car. And she was right. She could hear Evan's voice as she approached the salon.

However, she was surprised to hear Philip's voice. In the few meals that she had shared with the family, she had observed that Philip never spoke loud enough to be heard except by those closest to him. Now he was positively shouting. Cecilia stopped in the hall, uncertain of what to do.

"You're making an issue of something that doesn't exist!" Philip was saying.

"Are you trying to tell me that this estate has not been plagued by malicious acts of sabotage for nearly a year?" It was Evan's voice.

"Accidents, Evan! We've suffered a number of *accidents*—"

"You call the destruction of the milking machines an

accident? You're a fool, Philip. That kind of 'accident' was deliberately calculated to undermine the health of our herd—priceless stock, Philip—and to damage our reputation with the processing firms we engage. It may take days to—"

"Not days. You're exaggerating. I've already arranged to rent machines from—"

"Rent machines!" Evan railed. "The expense of renting that kind of equipment is going to cripple us."

"Evan, I know you have a head for money, and maybe I should just turn over the manor to you, but—"

"Philip, Philip, I don't want the manor. It's your inheritance—and Tony's—I'm concerned about. I'm trying to protect that by insisting you face reality. Someone is trying to destroy Chesterton!"

"Evan, I'll never to able to repay you for all you've done," Philip said with heavy resignation. "I don't know how you come up with the vast sums of money you generate to keep this place afloat, and I don't want to know. But I'm sure you're wrong about this sabotage theory of yours. You haven't been back at Chesterton long enough to. . . ."

Cecilia ran back down the great central hallway. This time she had been eavesdropping. She had listened to a conversation that she had no business hearing. She felt a rush of guilt and fear, then Evan's words floated into her mind.

Evan thought someone was trying to destroy Chesterton. That must be the stigma the manor held, she decided, the stigma that he would not discuss with her. And what had Philip meant when he said that Evan earned vast sums of money for the estate? As far as she could see, Evan didn't even have a job. She was trembling when she reached her suite, and as she closed the door noiselessly behind her she was grateful that she would have the afternoon to compose herself before facing the family for dinner.

GRADUALLY THE NERVOUSNESS IN HER VOICE lessened as Cecilia walked from room to room in the east wing, repeating the lines she'd prepared for the first group of visitors to Chesterton the next day. She practiced her gestures and the way she would point to various items and found that she hardly had to refer to the notes she had written. The benefits of her long hours of effort on Sunday were beginning to show, she thought, pleased with herself.

When she'd reached the gallery, she suddenly stopped. Catherine was standing at the far end of the immense room, directly facing the wall. Cecilia could not imagine what she could be doing, but Catherine gave her no time to speculate. Almost instantly she turned around, as if she were nervous and sensed Cecilia's presence.

"Why, Cecilia," she smiled broadly, beginning to walk the length of the gallery to Cecilia's side. "I'm so glad we met. I've been looking for an opportunity to compliment you on how accomplished you've become. Every time I hear you practicing I'm more impressed."

"Thank you," Cecilia smiled. In the three days she had spent at the manor Catherine had been the most consistently pleasant member of the family. She was always exquisitely dressed, and she never failed to smile brightly and say precisely the right thing.

"You must have noted that our family gatherings can become a trifle self-centered," she continued easily, "and of course, I can't help but be caught up in the affairs of Chesterton. But I have been meaning to have a chat with you."

"That's very kind of you," replied Cecilia. "I don't really feel that I know any of you very well. And I'm not one to intrude," she added, trying to wipe out the memory of the conversation between Evan and his brother that she'd listened to.

"Cecilia, dear," Catherine crooned, "you're one of the family now, and I hope to make you feel right at home here."

Cecilia was vaguely grated by the smoothness of Catherine's delivery at this close range. In the family gatherings she had appeared to be the only relaxed and happy person present. But here, apart from the others, the effect was different.

"You must be looking forward to your son's homecoming," Cecilia offered.

"Oh, yes. It will be splendid to see Tony again. But," Catherine continued with a little ripple of laughter, "as you will see, Tony is my stepson. He's eleven years old! And I don't really think I look old enough yet to be his mother!"

"I had no idea how old he was," Cecilia said quickly, laughing along with Catherine at her mistake.

"And naturally his father is looking forward to seeing him, though I can't imagine why he's gardening today. He'll greet the boy with those eternally grass-stained knees if I don't get after him." There was a hint of sharpness to her voice as she finished speaking.

"His Lordship enjoys gardening?"

"I presume so," Catherine replied. "He does it constantly. It's his contribution, you see, to the upkeep of the manor. We have no gardener on staff."

"He must be very talented to maintain those formal gardens," Cecilia observed.

"Oh, he is!" Catherine insisted with a toss of her luxurious blond hair. "He is. A perfect dear, my Philip."

Cecilia could not think of a way to reply to Catherine's gushing tribute to her husband. And although she was not exactly on her guard, she didn't feel inclined to ask Catherine to clear up any of the questions that were so often on her mind. Catherine, however, made it unnecessary for her to carry the conversation.

"Of course, we all do our part for Chesterton, as you must have gathered. Lovely Emily is wonderfully talented musically. Bless her, she works very hard giving piano lessons throughout the region. Oh, the money isn't much, but it's the thought, you know."

"And Evan?" Cecilia could not resist saying.

"I don't know what Evan does," Catherine said, a trifle harshly. "Obviously he manages the tours. And he has a lofty degree from Cambridge in art history and is supposed to be writing a book in that private study of his."

"Really?" Cecilia said wonderingly. "A book?"

"It might better be titled 'Gamblers I Have Known' than 'Art Through the Ages,' as far as I can see!" Catherine went on hotly. "I don't know why Philip doesn't put his foot down. Evan is a veritable legend, you know, in all the smoky rooms of society gamblers.

And Philip is allowing him to live here at Chesterton while he cleans out the county of Devonshire and pretends to write a book! Evan maintains his own income—and supports that beastly horse Tchaikovsky—and Philip thinks it's all just fine because he contributes some money to the Chesterton accounts."

"I haven't had a chance to visit the stables," Cecilia put in. "Tchaikovsky is Emily's horse, isn't he?"

"Emily's nemesis," Catherine corrected. "The reason the poor girl limps so pitifully is that monster horse's fault. She had a terrible accident not a year ago and was in bed for months—*months*! Her leg was broken in so many places that the best doctors in all of Britain couldn't prevent the leg from healing an inch shorter for the ordeal. Yet still she insists on keeping that beast! The animal ought to be shot! There's not a soul who would dare ride him!"

Cecilia was intrigued by the controversy surrounding Tchaikovsky. She had missed terribly the opportunity to ride since she'd left the preserve. "How many other horses are there in the stables?" she inquired hopefully.

Catherine was prevented from replying by the entrance of Gwen. She fixed her crystalline blue eyes on the girl the moment she saw her, and Gwen appeared to steel herself for an unpleasant encounter.

"So sorry to interrupt, your Ladyship," she began, "but Lady Emily has gone off to collect Master Tony at the station. I thought I'd best report to you about the preparations for his arrival."

"You should report to me in any case," Catherine replied stiffly. "Do excuse me, Cecilia. I really must go and check that everything has been done properly for Tony's homecoming dinner."

"Of course," Cecilia said, though she felt a pang of sympathy for little Gwen as she watched her trailing Catherine.

As she stood there, a familiar question nagged at her. Where on earth had she seen Catherine before? The question would not leave her mind, but nor could she answer it.

IN THE SOFT CANDLELIGHT everyone at the table looked happy and relaxed. Emily and Gwen had prepared a beautiful feast for Tony's homecoming, and Cecilia was touched to see how deeply the young boy appreciated the attention. He was, in Cecilia's eyes, a perfect child, and he had inherited the best of the Cedric-Browne features. He had his father's warm brown eyes and Evan's clear, perfectly proportioned features. Yet his coloring must have come from his mother, she decided, for his head was a mass of silky red curls. Cecilia found it hard to understand how his father could bear to send him away for nine months of the year, but as she observed the interaction of the family she received subtle clues that helped her to form a conclusion.

Although Catherine did not spare the boy her gushing charms, Tony was clearly not taken with his step-mother. And his quick wit and talkative manner did not seem to mesh well with the quiet self-effacing pose that his father always maintained. Tony's first loyalties obviously lay with Emily, who seemed more a second mother to him than an aunt. Evan, too, was clearly important to him.

As for herself, Cecilia could not help but note that she had received more notice from the young center of attention than she had received in all the days she'd spent with the adults of the Cedric-Browne family.

"I bet I know what we're having for dessert," Tony said happily. "And I bet Cecilia never tasted anything like it in Africa."

Cecilia laughed at the boy's anticipation of the unnamed treat. "What have I never tasted?" she inquired of him with a smile.

"It's got cake and custard and jam and cr-e-a-m," Tony began, stretching out his description with glee. "And sherry," he continued suggestively. "And it comes in a big bowl, and it's sweet and heavy and light and—"

"And it's like nothing I've ever heard of," Cecilia laughed.

"Why, it's a sherry trifle, silly," Tony cried. "Aunt Emily makes the best trifle in the world. She uses Chesterton cream. You do know about our cream, don't you, Cecilia?"

"I know that Devonshire is renowned for its dairy products," she answered.

"Double-clotted cream, though," Tony insisted. "That's what's special. I don't know if I'd be able to give up cream—even to see all the elephants you've seen."

"I'm sure it'd be a hard decision," Cecilia said seriously. "Do you know what they make butter out of in Africa?"

Tony shook his head.

"Buffalo milk," Cecilia informed him.

Tony made a face. "There's nothing like a Jersey

cow," he insisted. "We learned all about them in school, and when I grow up—"

"Dessert!" called Gwen, obviously as pleased as everyone else to have Tony home. She placed the masterful sherry trifle in front of Tony briefly before removing it to serve the individual portions. To Cecilia's surprise, Tony was actually able to manage a second helping of the rich dessert, but he showed himself to be an unusually thoughtful young gentleman, for he insisted that the piece be cut so as to insure Gwen a sizable portion of the sweet.

After the meal was over Tony took Emily by the hand and began to beg her to play the piano for him. Emily happily complied. Catherine said that she had several letters to write, and Evan explained simply that he had an engagement. While Philip did not seem to have any pressing plans, Cecilia wasn't inclined to spend a dull hour chatting with him after the festive dinner. She had decided that Philip was completely lacking in personality; though he was always kindly, he was never interesting. And Cecilia had plans of her own.

IT WAS ONLY A SHORT WALK to the stable, and the path was easy to follow by the light of the setting sun. The family had dined at seven this evening instead of at eight, in expectation of Tony's fatigue from the excitement of the day. Cecilia had quickly changed out of her dinner dress into a pair of melon-colored culottes with a matching sleeveless blouse. She was delighted to be on her way to the stable.

Her father had insisted that his daughter learn to ride at an early age, maintaining that as long as she explored on horseback she would always be able to extricate herself from trouble. In Kenya, Cecilia had known many horses.

And she had seen a few horses that simply could not be broken, but they were very few. Experience had taught her that with patience and skill, almost any animal could be tamed, and she had had some bizarre pets while she was growing up. She was looking forward to meeting the "monster," Tchaikovsky.

Reaching the edge of the formal garden, Cecilia could see the beginning of the stable just thirty feet to her left. Gwen had pointed out the building from the windows of the gallery when it had been raining the day before, and Cecilia had been impressed by its size, even at a distance.

She was just about to cover the short space remaining when she spotted Catherine coming around the corner of the building. She was closely escorted by a man Cecilia recognized instantly as Mathias, the groom. Gwen had described him glowingly to her, saying that she had never spoken to him but that he was "the most handsomest man" she had ever laid eyes on.

The sight of Catherine and Mathias together made Cecilia hesitate. But when they stopped walking, so did Cecilia.

Catherine and Mathias were locked in a tight embrace.

Chapter 5

Cecilia's brow furrowed in frustration. She could not stop herself from glaring at the sharp-faced little boy standing in the front of the tour group she was taking through the east wing. With grim satisfaction, she noted that the child's parents were deeply embarrassed by their son's unruly behavior.

"But I want to know what it was like!" the little boy shouted with a stamp of his foot. "Was there any blood? Did he cry? This lady is a crummy guide!"

Cecilia felt her patience snap. She had spent a sleepless night worrying about Catherine and Mathias, about Evan's unexplained sources of income, about the "stigma" of Chesterton Manor and about the thieves that might at any time make an assault on the very wing in which she slept. Taking visitors through the first tour had made her more nervous than she had suspected it would. And now this brat was asking her to give a ghoulish description of the death of the sixth earl of

Chesterton. Cecilia found it hard to resist the temptation not to oblige.

"Lady Eleanora dressed in her most alluring gown on the night of the murder," Cecilia began in a hushed voice. "The very gown in which you see her there," she said, pointing at the brilliant painting on the gallery wall. "She entered Lord Chesterton's study with a silver tray bearing two snifters of brandy, the aroma of the rich liquor already gathering around the narrowed tops of the crystal glasses. And with a bewitching smile, she handed the fatal drink to her husband, the sixth earl of Chesterton."

The child's eyes widened as Cecilia leaned down and spoke directly to him.

"He took a sip of the brandy, savoring its heady bouquet, which masked the bitter taste of the deadly crystalline drug—strychnine. He gulped greedily from the glass of death, and then Lady Eleanora watched as her husband agonized through violent convulsions and unspeakable pain."

The boy rushed to hide behind his mother's back, and Cecilia stopped. She was instantly ashamed of the way she had terrorized the child, but she could not help remarking the faces of the others in the group. Several were clearly fascinated, but most of the expressions before her showed deep satisfaction.

Cecilia felt almost justified by the crowd's reaction—until she saw Emily in the doorway. Guilt at once returned. A stunt such as that could mean losing her job, she told herself, though she was too far away to see if Emily's face showed censure or . . . or an understanding of what had gone before. How long had she been listening?

The answer came soon enough. Cecilia escorted the group to the exit, bidding them goodbye and receiving a sizable tip from the embarrassed father of the troublesome youngster. Then, just as she was turning to go back to the front of the manor to receive the next group of waiting visitors, Emily appeared in her path.

"I hope you don't think—" Cecilia began her apology.

"I think you did splendidly," Emily said promptly. "That child deserved exactly what he got. I know I don't have the patience to deal with the perverted curiosities of the people who come here to feast on tragedy."

Cecilia sighed and leaned back against the wall. "I'm so glad you're not angry," she breathed. "I know I should have showed more patience, but . . . ."

"You have to keep your sanity, Cecilia," Emily said seriously. "Sometimes people will stand in the way of that. But take it from a wise old maid: only you can protect yourself. No matter how trivial the assault may seem—even from a little boy you don't know—always stand your ground. Because that's the only way you'll keep that sweet innocent disposition of yours. By never letting anyone get . . . get a chance to take it from you."

Cecilia was stunned by the vehemence of Emily's speech and by the fact that Emily—at probably no more than twenty-eight years of age—considered herself an old maid. Something terrible, Cecilia guessed, much more terrible than a riding accident, had happened to Emily, and the shifting currents of her personality were unfathomable. Desperately Cecilia struggled to think of a response that would lead Emily to tell her more, but the woman was once again drawing away.

"I won't keep you," Emily said in a monotone. "I have

my late-morning lessons to attend to." With that, she turned and limped toward the back of the wing, her stack of music resting heavily in the crook of her arm.

SLOWLY HER SLENDER HANDS EXPLORED the gleaming walnut paneling. Her eyes searched the grain of the wood and the graceful fluting of the molding. Cecilia had no idea what might be special about this stretch of wall at the far end of the gallery, but when no tourists had appeared for the noon tour she'd decided to come upstairs and examine the spot where Catherine had been standing the day before. Something in Catherine's manner when she'd first turned around had been off-key, and Cecilia was determined to discover why.

Suddenly powerful hands gripped her arms and swung her around from the wall. Cecilia found herself staring directly into Evan's angry face, his bushy eyebrows drawn in a frown that could not obscure the fury in his green eyes.

"Don't you ever go near that wall!" he ordered, not releasing his viselike grip. "Do you understand me?"

"No," Cecilia flared, "I don't! Let me go! You're hurting me!"

Evan's hands instantly dropped. "I'm sorry," he repeated, his tone soft and full of self-condemnation. "I wanted to protect you, and I guess I—"

"Protect me!" Cecilia exclaimed, refusing to let herself be moved by Evan's tender tone. "Protect me! Well, you might begin by telling me exactly what I need to be protected from."

Evan turned his back to Cecilia so that she could barely hear his next sentence. "This is a very old building. It was constructed at a time when—"

"Please, at least do me the courtesy of speaking *to* me," Cecilia demanded. "And I don't need a history of the manor. Why did you attack me?"

Evan now turned to face her. "It was constructed at a time when people's needs and motives were different from what they are today," he resumed evenly. "And there are a number of carefully concealed trapdoors, some of them exceedingly dangerous because they drop off suddenly into hidden corridors and chutes—"

"Why haven't you boarded them up from the inside?" Cecilia interrupted. "If they're so dangerous, it strikes me as highly irresponsible—"

"No one wants to detract from the authenticity of—"

"Another lie," Cecilia accused. Angrily she twisted her fingers in the thick, dark mass of hair gathered by a white ribbon at the nape of her neck.

Evan simply responded to Cecilia's accusation with silence. At first he appeared to want to say something, but instead he only gazed at her with the weary expression she'd come to associate with him. Perhaps Catherine was right about Evan's gambling life, Cecilia thought wonderingly. Perhaps he had secrets connected with whatever lay behind those trapdoors. . . .

"Cecilia," Evan said at last. "I came up here to tell you that you should feel free to exercise a little flexibility. If before lunch or dinner you find that no one has appeared, indicate on the tour sign that the next tour will be given either after lunch or the following morning. And take the time for yourself. Today, as it happens, I'm free. I thought I'd invite you to the garden."

Cecilia shook her head in dismay. It was happening again. He was going to pretend that the interchange about the trapdoors had never taken place, that she had never accused him of being a liar or demanded an explanation. She studied him for a moment. To her chagrin, she found that she was more intrigued by the prospect of taking a walk through the garden with him than angered at being dissuaded from discovering the truth. Quickly, she rationalized that she might be able to find out more from him in a moment of calm than she had in her anger. Nodding her consent to the walk, she and Evan made their way down the back stairway in silence.

As they approached the back door, Cecilia suddenly grabbed Evan's hand. She let out a small cry and pointed with her other hand to the window just to the left of the doorway.

The small window was filled with the face of a man she had never seen before. The man had wiry black hair covering his ears, and obscuring his face was a full black beard. His eyes met Evan's for an instant before he ducked out of sight.

Evan squeezed Cecilia's hand, then said quickly, "There's no need for you to worry. An associate of mine seems to have arrived unexpectedly. But I'm afraid we must defer our stroll through Philip's exquisite gardens."

THE CONVERSATION at lunch was as all the others had been, and Cecilia found it impossible to listen or to appear interested. Evan was not present, a fact that disturbed her greatly. She simply could not begin to make sense of her feelings about him. She told herself that she was a fool to trust him, but deep inside she knew that her foolishness was of a more serious nature. She was afraid that she was falling in love with him. And yet she had no experience of love. No, an inner voice insisted, she was only letting her imagination create exciting fantasies in which she would somehow come to the rescue of this troubled man, saving him from. . .from what?

Cecilia knew she had no right to ask him. She must resign herself to the fact that she had stumbled onto a strange household that basically was none of her concern. It didn't matter how Evan spent his time or earned his money. It didn't matter what might be happening at Chesterton or what may have happened to Emily in the past to make her so bitter. Cecilia decided that when the tourist season was over she would return to London with experience as a tour guide and seek employment with one of the big companies operating year round in the city. She would just have to endure the peculiarities of the Cedric-Brownes and their rudeness while she sought to build her own future.

Cecilia suddenly became aware of the fact that someone was addressing her. It was Tony. He was the only one ever to include her in a family conversation She listened to the earnest questions of the boy for a moment, then realized that he was speaking about the apple orchard. Apparently Emily had been rebuking her brother, Philip, for not attending to some trees that had become diseased. Now Tony was asking if there were apple trees in Kenya and if she had ever tasted fresh Devonshire cider. Cecilia was moved by how seriously

Tony had attempted to inform himself about his inheritance. She tried to respond cheerfully, but even Tony could see that she was troubled and soon stopped questioning her.

THERE WAS A SPRING in Cecilia's step as she walked through the garden in the early-evening sun, determined this time to see the stable and the controversial Tchaikovsky. The afternoon tours had gone surprisingly well, given the mood in which she had approached them after the scene with Evan and the thoughts she'd had over lunch. She was pleased to have handled the capacity crowds so skillfully, and when no one had arrived for the last tour of the day by five-forty, she had decided to take Evan's advice and close up early.

The luxuriant fragrance of roses from the far end of the garden greeted her, and she paused briefly to admire the many varieties that Philip had so artfully intermixed. Their delicate petals were deceptively hardy, for the hot summer sun had done nothing to diminish their rich regal beauty.

Taking a last deep breath of the roses, Cecilia exited from the boxwood-hedged garden and continued down the path to the stable. The familiar and beloved scent of horses now filled her nostrils, and she felt a flush of excitement.

But coming up to the stable doors, she faltered. The paint on the stable facade was peeling, and pieces of equipment cluttered the right of the entrance. One saddle was resting askew against the outside wall, and by all appearances, it had been there through several seasons. The neglect angered Cecilia, for though paint was costly and the family was supposed to be short on funds, carelessness could be even more costly. It was plain to see that the saddle was of high quality, and equally plain that it could now be restored only at considerable expense.

The picture inside the stable was equally disturbing. Cecilia saw four horses in rickety stalls directly in front of her. Around her, the room was in considerable disarray. The animals' food was scattered about haphazardly, and a large cistern of fetid water in the corner was attracting flies.

With growing disgust, Cecilia walked over to the stalls. Three of the horses were of average breeding, but it was a simple matter to determine that the fourth was the feared and prized Tchaikovsky. The massive mahogany thoroughbred shifted restlessly from hoof to hoof in the filthy stall, his magnificent muscles twitching in cadence with his nervous movements.

Cecilia rested her hands quietly on the door of the stall. Instantly the great head snapped to face her. Tchaikovsky's ears flattened against his head, and his sparkling black eyes fixed a menacing stare on her.

"You're a wild one, aren't you?" Cecilia whispered. "Beautiful, too."

The horse raised his head a shade, and a dangerous glint appeared in his eyes.

"I'll bet you've never had anyone understand you," Cecilia continued in an even, quiet voice. "But I think you and I could be friends."

Without a second thought she slid free the wooden bolt on the stall door and stepped inside. The horse was stilled momentarily by her unexpected entrance, but his ears remained flattened and his eyes continued to flash threateningly.

"There, there, boy. Relax now. Don't do anything unkind to your new friend," Cecilia crooned, patting him on the neck.

The massive head whipped around, and a swift snapping sound broke the silence in the stall. Only years of experience saved Cecilia from the fierce bite of the angry animal. But her steady purposeful retreat had placed her in the rear of the stall. She'd have to employ all her cleverness to calm the horse enough so that she could pass safely to the outside.

"Oh, my God!"

Cecilia looked across the stall door at the white terror-stricken face of Mathias.

"Get out of there or it's your life, you idiot!" he shouted. "What kind of a damn fool stunt—"

"Shut up," ordered Cecilia in a measured tone. "Don't you know better than to shout in the presence of an agitated horse?"

"He's a beast," Mathias retorted angrily. "And you risked my job going in that—"

"I asked you to lower your voice," Cecilia interrupted, not taking her eyes off Tchaikovsky. "This is one of the most noble horses I've ever laid eyes on, and someone *should* have your job for allowing him to get into this condition."

"Well, I'll be damned, you haughty—" Mathias suddenly stopped talking. Out of the corner of her eye, Cecilia saw why. Emily and Tony had come into the stable—exactly when, she couldn't say—and Mathias had just realized that they were only a few feet away.

"Lady Emily," he began apologetically, "I had no idea you—"

"Never mind, Mathias," Emily hissed. "Get Miss Bennett out of that stall without mishap—and without any further insult."

Cecilia rapidly calculated the dangers. One false move and the enormous weight of the horse would squash her against the back wall of the stall. Tchaikovsky's head snapped again, but this time he was only inches off the mark. And Cecilia had no room to maneuver. The moment had come.

"Mathias," Cecilia said authoritatively, "open that door. Exactly ten inches—no more, no less. And hold it steady."

Mathias did as he was told.

Lifting her right arm slowly, Cecilia kept her eyes locked with those of the enraged Tchaikovsky. When her hand was raised to full height she brought it down swiftly with all her might on the horse's rump. Startled by this sudden move, Tchaikovsky jumped slightly to one side.

Cecilia slipped out of the stall before the horse had recovered, but as she slid the bolt home Tchaikovsky reared up and neighed viciously.

"Oh, Cecilia!" Tony cried. "I've never seen anyone who could outsmart Tchaikovsky!"

"You do know your horses, Miss Bennett," Mathias said uneasily. "I'm the groom and I've never been able to do anything with that devil. But you'd best stay clear of him while luck's on your side."

Cecilia eyed Mathias coldly. She had no doubt that his incompetence had all but ruined a magnificent animal. Yet even in her anger and excitement she couldn't help but notice that Mathias had assumed a challenging self-assured stance.

"Too many people have obviously stayed clear of him," Cecilia rejoined hotly. "And you are the worst offender—a man who is employed to take care of the stock, and this is the result!"

"You will never go near Tchaikovsky again." It was Emily's voice, flat and resolute, coming from the shadow to Cecilia's left. "Tchaikovsky has chosen a life of solitude," she continued slowly, "and he protects that solitude in whatever way he can. And you, Mathias," she concluded icily, "will say nothing of this incident to anyone. Nothing. And that's an order."

Emily turned and walked stiffly from the stable, her limp the only thing detracting from the intense dignity of her pose. Tony rushed after her.

Cecilia glanced at Mathias, then around at Tchaikovsky. In an instant her decision was made. She had to catch up with Emily and Tony.

On nimble feet she dashed out of the ill-kept stable after them, but they were already out of sight. Then she heard Emily's sobs. Following the sound, she found Emily and Tony in the woods just behind the stable.

Emily was sitting on a fallen log, crying as if the world had come to an end. Tony knelt before her, trying to comfort her.

"What's the—I don't understand..." Cecilia stammered in confusion. One minute Emily had been rock hard, speaking without a shred of emotion, and now she seemed utterly fragile.

"Oh, of course you don't understand," Emily sobbed.

"How could you? But that's no excuse for your sticking your head in where you—"

"Aunt Emily, don't you see?" Tony was pleading. "Cecilia might be able to tame Tchaikovsky, and then—"

"Nobody can tame him," Emily insisted. "And when Philip and Catherine find out...it's all over. He's lost."

"But Philip and Catherine won't find out," Cecilia interjected. "None of us will say anything, and you ordered Mathias—"

"I ordered Mathias," Emily groaned. "Open your eyes, Cecilia. Accept the damage you have done."

Suddenly Cecilia remembered the scene between Catherine and Mathias that she had witnessed just on the previous evening. Could Emily know what was going on between her sister-in-law and the groom? And if she did, why had she chosen to keep silent? In any case, it was not something she could pursue in Tony's presence. But she had one more idea.

"If we told Evan, then perhaps he could—"

"Please, Cecilia," Emily begged through her tears, "stay out of it! And don't tell Evan. His burdens are far too great as it is."

"I'm sorry," Cecilia said sincerely. "I didn't mean to hurt you." Then, sensing that there was nothing more she could say to calm her, Cecilia quietly slipped from the tiny grove, taking with her a strangely reassuring parting glance from Tony.

His burdens are far too great as it is. The words echoed in her mind as she hurried back to the privacy of her suite. Emily's words confirmed what she herself had sensed: that Evan was acting oddly out of some nameless devotion . . . to another woman? Cecilia couldn't be certain—nor did she want to be.

What was clear to her was that there were strange alliances in this household, ruling the undercurrents of tension she'd felt since her arrival. As well, there was definitely something happening between Catherine and Mathias that could not be denied. And Cecilia doubted that it was in Philip's best interests.

But beyond these observations, Cecilia was beginning to see that there was a deep and loving bond among Evan, Emily and Tony. And she felt drawn to all of them. She couldn't remain aloof from their lives. She was positive now that her plan would help them. Tomorrow morning she would put it into action.

Chapter 6

The night breezes blew soft summer air into the pleasant sitting room, and Cecilia put her book aside to fully enjoy the evening. So far the week had been one of successes, she mused. The very morning after the upsetting incident with Tchaikovsky, she had begun to enact her plan.

Shortly before dawn she had stolen down to the stable and found it deserted. Again she had approached the magnificent Tchaikovsky, but this time she had calculated each move carefully, taking advantage of the fact that the horse was still somewhat groggy from sleep.

Cecilia was horrified to discover that Tchaikovsky had been brutally beaten. The scars of old and fresh whip marks marred his smooth flanks, and from the angle of the lashes, Cecilia was able to determine that the offender was strong—and cowardly. Someone had evidently sat high up on the back railing of the stall and

leveled the blows mercilessly on the confined animal.
This piece of guesswork only made Cecilia's task easier.
It told her that Tchaikovsky had not been bred into his
present vicious state but rather driven there. In a horse
of his age such damage could be corrected.

That first morning Cecilia had placed a saddle on his
back and led him around the stable yard. Though the
sun had barely broken over the horizon, she could feel
the beads of sweat forming on her brow. If she failed . . .
but she didn't dare imagine the consequences of failure.
Surprisingly, Tchaikovsky had accepted her. The first
battle was won.

In the days that followed, Cecilia had been able to
make Tchaikovsky comfortable with her as his rider.
And this morning, as always just at dawn, she and
Tchaikovsky had made their longest trip. She had ridden him through the fragrant apple orchards, certain
that the horse had enjoyed the excursion as much as she
had. The earlier tenseness was all but gone in both rider
and horse.

Now Cecilia was faced with the decision of when to
tell the Cedric-Brownes of her accomplishment. She
closed her eyes and imagined the possible scenarios. All
of them involved a trial. Further, the trial would have to
include the success of another rider, for it hardly mattered that one tour guide hired for a season had
mastered the beast. No, Tchaikovsky had to be ready to
accept any rider, even the inexperienced Tony. And for
Cecilia to be confident about that she would need to
keep her secret for another week.

Cecilia suddenly smiled. The tours had gone well,
too. Emily had told her that the hotels and restaurants

in Dartmouth sent out scouts every year so that they could recommend exceptional attractions in the area. The effects of the scouts' reports were already showing, and she hadn't had a moment's rest in the past three days, it seemed. In each half-hour period on the tour days, Cecilia had led a full group through the east wing. Each day she had placed the day's earnings in the strongbox that Evan had provided.

Tonight she had counted the money in amazement. She'd never guessed that the tours could generate so much income. It would be gratifying to turn over the entire week's sum to Evan the next day, knowing that it was so large because she herself had done well.

Cecilia glanced at her watch. Just after eleven. She ought to be getting to bed, she thought, yet she didn't want to end the luxury of these moments of quiet reflection.

Only two things had detracted from the week's happiness. Well, maybe three. But she shouldn't even be considering the third, she decided with a twinge of regret.

The most important incident was definitely the one that had taken place at luncheon the day after the scene in the stable. Mathias had wasted no time in contravening Emily's order and had reported the entire story directly to Catherine. The ensuing argument was the most rancorous Cecilia had witnessed in many years.

Catherine had lashed out at Emily for her continued blindness in the face of all the damning evidence against the horse's temperament. She had even threatened to punish Tony for not coming to her at once and telling her what had happened. Moreover, she had nearly convinced Philip that the time for sale had come.

Cecilia had listened in embarrassed dismay to the argument that her own actions had created. If the horse were sold, she knew instinctively that Emily would never recover emotionally. If only she could think of something to say that would buy her the time she needed to train Tchaikovsky! Cecilia sensed it would be sheer folly to reveal so soon the fact that she'd already begun to tame him, and her sense of decorum would not let her enter into the family argument.

She had been ready to excuse herself from the battleground of the table when Evan had stepped forcefully into the fray. Cecilia had seen him exert his power over the family before, but she wasn't prepared for the methods he employed on this occasion. She could still hear his strong domineering voice as he took control.

"Cecilia," he had said, looking her straight in the eye, "what is the extent of your experience with horses?"

Cecilia swallowed and summoned her courage to participate in the argument. "I've been around scores of horses most of my life. I was covering some of the most difficult terrain in Africa on horseback by the age of eleven. I wouldn't even try to estimate how many horses I've helped to break." Cecilia was pleased with herself. She had said it. And it was all true.

"And what is your opinion of Tchaikovsky?"

"Tchaikovsky is the most wonderful horse I've ever seen," she replied, feeling the daggers in Catherine's blue eyes trained on her.

"If he were your horse as he is Emily's, would you sell him?"

"No," Cecilia said simply. She could see Tony suppressing a happy smile at these words.

"Would you consider Tchaikovsky to be dangerous?" Evan went on.

Cecilia paused before answering. She knew it wouldn't be safe for just anyone to approach the animal. Yet she couldn't allow him to be sold. Everything depended on her answer—which had to be honest.

"At the moment," she said slowly, "Tchaikovsky is not in any condition to be approached by a novice. A lion cub can be safe and delightful if approached by the right person, or terribly dangerous in the wrong hands. Like the cub, Tchaikovsky requires the respect of an experienced hand. Given that, I'd say he's totally safe."

Evan's response to this carefully phrased answer took Cecilia by surprise. She'd half hoped that he would invite her to train Tchaikovsky. Then she could have proceeded openly. But Evan had spoken with finality, saying that Tchaikovsky would stay—and that when he himself had the time he would see to hiring a proper trainer.

Cecilia shuddered slightly. What would Evan say when he learned that she'd taken it upon herself to be that trainer? But as she pushed this unpleasant question out of her mind, the second disturbing event of that week came to take its place.

Cecilia closed her eyes for a moment, mentally seeing a gray-eyed man's face. He had been in the tour group twice the day before and once today, but he didn't strike her as a tourist. The man was of medium height with sandy blond hair, and he had the hands of a man who worked outdoors. No camera was slung over his shoulder, nor did he carry the usual sack of tourist accoutrements containing everything from guidebooks to candy and picnic lunches. Further, he didn't seem interested in Cecilia's description of the manor.

What troubled Cecilia was that she couldn't figure out why he came to the manor. He had studied her intently on the first day, a fact she'd been well aware of, and that had fixed him in her mind. But after that his eyes had wandered from treasure to treasure as if other thoughts strongly occupied his mind.

Was he one of the ring of thieves currently looting the Devonshire countryside, Cecilia wondered uneasily. Could he be calculating, assessing, and planning for an assault on Chesterton? Was it possible that such a quiet honest-looking man could be involved in criminal activities?

Cecilia could not bring herself to draw any conclusions. Something was troubling the man deeply; perhaps Chesterton had become a kind of refuge for him. Just as some people sit through the same movie time and again to give themselves privacy, perhaps this man had chosen the historic beauty of the manor.

Still, Cecilia was worried. She knew, too, that she should tell Evan about him, just in case. It was a problem for her employer to solve, not her. And after all, who was she to think that she could spot a criminal?

Evan.... The third disturbing matter of that week centered on him. Cecilia couldn't prevent herself from counting him on her list.

Evan had been absent at both dinner and lunch several times in the past few days. His absences went completely unexplained, and no one even remarked on them. Cecilia suspected that his actions weren't those of a man quietly writing a book on art history. He had been away from the manor, she was positive.

At first Cecilia had tried to tell herself that he was the no-good gambler Catherine had claimed he was and that he must be off gambling. But another possibility had seemed more persuasive. Cecilia felt certain that he was secretly engaged in some activity for the nameless "person who was dear to him."

But could another woman really be the cause of Evan's absences, she wondered unhappily. The very words implied that she, Cecilia, was a woman in his life. And that was preposterous, she told herself sternly. No, the reason that his absences had disturbed her was very simple. She missed him. She felt lonely and out of place when he wasn't at the table. True, he was invariably tense, occasionally even rude, at the family gatherings, but Cecilia now felt she could see beyond his abruptness at such times.

On a few precious occasions she had met him by chance in the manor. There had never been much time for them to talk, but he had struck her as a different and thoroughly likable man once away from the others. He'd always shown a genuine interest in how she was faring, displaying an easy sense of humor that radiated both kindness and sensitivity.

More than anything else, Cecilia looked forward to the possibility of another chance meeting with Evan Cedric-Browne. At last she'd had to admit why. She was in love with him—and she knew she was a complete fool. Evan and her feelings for him had somehow become the third disturbing item on her list.

Cecilia reached over and extinguished the light. If she

didn't get some sleep, she told herself, Tchaikovsky would sense her weakness the next morning, and her work might be set back by days. Cecilia stood up and began to thread her way carefully through the darkness to the bedroom door, but the sound of a car outside caused her to stop abruptly.

Curious, Cecilia picked her way through the darkness to the window. But what she saw instantly made her wish she'd long since gone to bed.

Behind the wheel of his black Morris Minor sat Evan. The light was switched on briefly inside the car, and she noticed that in spite of the summer weather he was dressed in black. The light went off quickly, and a strange man suddenly appeared in the headlights. Flashing the inside light, Cecilia guessed, must have been a signal, given to the woods farthest from the family quarters. The man in the headlights was dressed entirely in black, too, his clothes blending with the wiry blackness of his hair and beard. Cecilia suddenly recognized him. It was the same man who'd unexpectedly arrived the day that she'd agreed to take a stroll with Evan. But what was he doing on a summer's eve at midnight?

GWEN BEAMED. "Don't you look lovely!" she exclaimed pleasantly. "That pretty pink dress brings out the roses in your cheeks like the sun brings on the day!"

"You ought to be a poet, Gwen," Cecilia laughed. "Or a professional flatterer."

Gwen set down the usual breakfast tray of tea, toast, butter and marmalade, then straightened her small white cap. "I'm not one to be tellin' tales, Miss Bennett," she said with mock seriousness. "You're a picture. And what a pleasure it is to have a surprise for you today."

"For me? A surprise?"

"Now, don't get overexcited," Gwen warned, reaching under the breakfast tray and extracting a newspaper. "The paperboy accidentally delivered two *Dartmouth Registers* instead of one. I took the extra copy for you, thinkin' you might enjoy a little local color with your breakfast."

"Why, Gwen, that is a pleasant surprise," Cecilia smiled.

Gwen seemed pleased. "Got to be on my way—Saturday's baking day 'round here," she sang.

"Don't work too hard," Cecilia called after her as she headed for the door.

"Not to worry," Gwen said, then winked before closing the door.

The instant Gwen had gone Cecilia poured herself a cup of tea, buttered a slice of toast and opened the newspaper. She raised the china cup to her lips but set it back in its saucer almost instantly without taking a sip. The headline hit her with the force of a scalding Kenya wind: Two Criminals Sought in Massive Art Theft.

As Cecilia's eyes traveled down the column she felt her heart start to race. Then she began to read the article more closely.

Benningsway House, home of the Honorable Ian St. James, was the scene last night of the biggest of the art-related heists in the current wave of robberies plaguing Devonshire. Witnesses reported seeing two men traveling at high speed from the area shortly after 2:00 A.M. Though no clear descriptions were possible, both are believed to have been dressed in black. Authorities are pursuing all leads.

Owner St. James speculated that the thieves were well informed, as they passed over items of lesser value in favor of a Gainsborough portrait, a Turner landscape, an Egyptian cartouche dating back to 1400 B.C., a rare tablet bearing cuneiform script. . . .

Trembling, Cecilia let the newspaper fall, her appetite lost. She closed her eyes, not wanting to believe the obvious. But all she could see was Evan's Morris Minor stopped briefly before her window while the black-bearded man rushed to climb into the passenger seat.

How could she have believed in Evan's integrity, she wondered despairingly. He had seemed like such a tower of strength in this strange household. And now...now she was alone again. As alone as she had felt on the day her father died.

THE GRAY-EYED MAN stared up at the portrait of Lady Eleanora while the other members of the tour group busied themselves by squinting down at the glass cases in the gallery. The last five minutes of the tour were devoted to a question period in which the visitors were encouraged to look at the various artifacts in the cases or pursue a particular point of interest with the guide, and most of them actively participated.

Cecilia walked directly over to the gray-eyed man. The minute she'd seen him she'd known he must be one of the criminals who had looted Benningsway the previous night. Still, a part of her rebelled against the idea. Yet it couldn't have been Evan and. . .and that man. If she could somehow implicate this mild-looking visitor, then she would be able to approach Evan with her discovery—and Evan would assure her of his own innocence.

"You seem to be inordinately interested in Chesterton Manor," Cecilia remarked.

The gray-eyed man turned to her and blinked. It was not until Cecilia was face to face with him that she realized the danger of her tactics. Inwardly she shuddered, knowing that she must build her case without letting the man guess her purpose. For if he were the thief. . . .

"Yes," the man replied forthrightly. "Yes, I am."

The answer put Cecilia at a loss. She had expected a denial, a remark designed to throw her from the truth. "Is there anything in particular that, uh, draws you to my tours?" she asked.

"Not really," he answered vaguely. "I simply. . .the place is full of. . .beauty." For the first time Cecilia saw that the man was a study in sadness. His misty eyes, the fine lines in his suntanned face, and the set of his jaw expressed a sadness incongruous with his age. He probably wasn't much older than thirty, Cecilia decided. Still, unhappiness and tragedy could come at any age. . . .

"The beauty of the art, perhaps," she probed, suddenly recalling her intent.

"The beauty of Chesterton," the man corrected.

"Surely there are other estates of historic note in the area that command your attention, as well?"

"Only Chesterton commands my attention," the man said sadly. "Do you find my continued presence at your tours distressing?"

"Oh, no," Cecilia replied without thinking. What was she saying? Of course she found his visits distressing. She only hoped that she had guessed the correct reason for them. Though to imagine this man a thief was still next to impossible for her—more so now that she had finally spoken with him. But she didn't want to discourage him from returning. He was still her only lead.

"I hope to see you often over the course of the summer," she said kindly. "And I hope you'll feel free to inquire about anything that particularly intrigues you." Cecilia thought she had probably just played right into the hands of a well-disguised criminal, yet she'd been unable to stop herself. The man had seemed so sincere that she didn't want to drive him away.

Suddenly he smiled, a thin melancholy smile. "Thank you," he said shyly. "The Cedric-Browne family ought not to let you go." His eyes fluttered back to the portrait of Lady Eleanora, and he added mysteriously, "I hope with all my heart that...that you will be allowed to... to stay. I'm sure you're needed here."

CECILIA WALKED BRISKLY down the central hallway. She had only a vague impression of where Evan's private study was located, but she was determined to find it without asking anyone for directions. When Evan had been absent at luncheon her suspicions had reached a fever pitch. She *had* to know if he'd robbed Benningsway House last night. Only Evan could answer that question, however indirectly.

She'd written a brief note to him explaining that the afternoon tours had brought a group of German tourists and that she'd been able to accommodate them by providing a bilingual version of her speech. Her note suggested that she and Evan should meet to discuss the possibility of formalizing a foreign-language tour program. The suggestion was a good one, she knew, but it was only a ploy. She wanted to have some time alone with Evan as soon as he returned to the manor, and the tours were the only subject that she felt she could approach him on.

Finding no one in the salon, Cecilia bounded up the steps of the curving staircase leading to the second floor. When she'd reached the landing she pulled the manor's floor plan out of her pocket and looked down the long row of doors. Evan had given her the floor plan on her first day here, along with all the other printed material about Chesterton. But she'd never dreamed that she would use it in this way.

Following the diagram, she turned to her right and proceeded down a dark corridor. There were only a few doors, and at the end of the hall she saw the door to Evan's study. Its brass handle gleamed even in the dim interior light, and the wood had a heavy ancient look to it. She heard nothing behind the door, and paused for only a second before slipping the handwritten message under the threshold. Then she scurried back to the elegant stairway. She knew she had no business being on the second floor of the west wing uninvited, and suddenly she found herself running back through the great central hallway of the ground floor. She wanted to be back in her own suite. She wanted. . . .

"Stop, Cecilia!" a woman's voice commanded.

Cecilia came to an immediate halt, but not before she had run directly into Catherine.

"Oh, Catherine," Cecilia gasped. "I'm so sorry. Did I hurt you?"

"Not a scratch," Catherine laughed. "But did someone hurt *you*?" she asked seriously. "You look as if you've just come from the scene of a hurricane."

"Oh, do I look that bad?" Cecilia said, smoothing her hair.

"No, you don't look that bad," Catherine smiled. "But whatever is the matter?"

"Nothing," Cecilia replied, trying to regain her composure. Catherine was not someone she wanted to confide in. "Just a busy day, you know. Lots of visitors, and I have the accounts to do. Hate being late for dinner." She was talking unnaturally, but she couldn't stop herself.

"Well, calm down, dear. Evan has no right to expect miracles. And you're not being paid to run everywhere you go."

"No, I guess not." Cecilia managed a smile. Her calm was returning. "But I really ought to be hurrying along. I have no head for figures and—"

"Well, I won't keep you," Catherine said soothingly. "But do take the time for a nice bath. That's precisely what I'm planning for myself at the moment."

Cecilia nodded and watched the other woman saunter off down the hallway. Catherine didn't seem to be in need of a relaxing bath, Cecilia thought in surprise. She looked as if she had just spent the afternoon sipping iced tea in the garden and reading the fashion magazines that were sticking out of the canvas bag she carried.

As she opened the door to her suite Cecilia wondered for the first time what Catherine's contribution to

Chesterton was supposed to be. Everyone was always talking about "contributions" to the flagging family resources. Perhaps Catherine felt that she was doing her part by keeping the groom happy. . . .

That was unkind, Cecilia rebuked herself. Although she didn't approve of Catherine's secret, she had to admit that the mistress of the house had never been anything except pleasant to her. How Philip and Catherine managed their marriage was certainly none of her business.

Cecilia walked over to the writing table and pulled out the oversize bottom drawer. Her business, she reminded herself, was to keep track of the money in the strongbox. She reached into the drawer and lifted the box. Instantly she knew something was wrong.

The box was open. And oddly light in weight.

She jerked the box out of the drawer and placed it on top of the desk, then threw open the metal lid. The box was empty! Obviously the lock had been picked. Worse, the entire week's earnings had been stolen.

Chapter 7

Cecilia could not begin to imagine who had taken the money. For several minutes she simply stared at the empty box, bewildered.

Finally she stood up shakily, but she couldn't stop trembling. The truth was inescapable. The stigma of Chesterton Manor had finally touched her.

Was this what had driven the other tour guides away, she wondered. Had they been accused of theft? Or had they simply been unable to bear up under the tension of the household? Had they told Evan, their employer, what was happening? Could that be a part of his theory that someone was trying to destroy the manor? There were just too many questions. She had to calm down and think through what had happened.

Absently Cecilia began to pace the length of the sitting room. As she walked, one point became clear to her: the thief was no stranger to Chesterton. She had not been gone from her room long enough for an outsider to enter, locate the box and pick its lock, then disappear unseen. The only logical conclusion was that one of the members of the family had stolen the money, Cecilia reasoned.

Yet the amount of money involved made the hypothesis unsound. A little more than a thousand dollars for the first five days.... It was hard to believe that such a sum could be meaningful to anyone living at Chesterton, given the risk of exposure. Despite all the talk of the financial state of the Cedric-Browne fortune, the family lived in style. To a poor man a thousand dollars might be enticing. But to a Cedric-Browne?

Cecilia couldn't accept that. No, the theft had to be only one small part of some master plan. How true it now seemed that the manor was "jinxed." Diseased orchards, neglected stables, malfunctioning milking machines, departing tour guides.... Nothing seemed to go smoothly at Chesterton.

But who would want to spoil the lovely estate? The name Catherine sprang instantly to her mind. Catherine had never shown any love of Chesterton. Yet the woman did love luxury, and it was difficult for Cecilia to imagine her plotting against the grandeur of the estate to which she now shared title.

Cecilia couldn't let her disapproval of Catherine's dealings with Mathias cloud her judgment. Even if the woman were having an affair with Mathias, that could not be used to implicate her as a thief, much less a saboteur.

Abruptly Cecilia stopped pacing. She had to decide what course of action she would now follow. More than a thousand dollars—money that had been entrusted to her—was missing. For a moment she tried to imagine what would happen if she simply told the truth. But she had been at the manor for such a short time, not enough time for her to have built up anyone's trust. Whoever the thief was would surely lobby for her dismissal, and she would leave Chesterton with only the grim satisfaction of knowing who had framed her. Worse, she would leave a failure, knowing she had done nothing to help the people she had come to care for—Tony and Emily...and Evan.

She sank down heavily into the bright yellow armchair before the fireplace and folded her legs under her. She desperately needed time to discover the truth and break the chain of events that was destroying the manor.

Cecilia had never walked away from hardship in her life. Although she had no complaints about the way she had been raised in Kenya, she knew that it had been a world in which conquests were imperative for survival—especially for a lone girl growing up away from all the normal comforts of modern life. The challenges of English life might be different, she reasoned, but Cecilia Bennett would not walk away without a fight.

Her mind made up, Cecilia dragged the bentwood desk chair over to the bookcase and kicked off her shoes. Standing on the chair and reaching as high as she could, she was able to reach the top shelf. Then, taking the books off the shelf two at a time, she began the laborious procedure of clearing the shelf in the deep, blond oak bookcase.

At last she had uncovered her money. Her own inheritance. Cecilia stared up at the stack of bills for a moment, then, without further pause, pulled off enough to replace the stolen tour money.

Barefoot, she padded across the soft wool carpet to the strongbox. The bills made a soft sound as she dropped them into the empty box. She would have to make up the exact sum.

She would tell Evan that she had been to the bank in Dartmouth and exchanged all the small bills for a few larger ones. Evan would believe her. But it was too soon for her to tell him the truth. She would have to collect more concrete evidence against the thief.

It wouldn't be easy, yet on that point time was on her side. The culprit wasn't likely to make another move where the tour money was concerned—not until Cecilia had collected another week's worth. In the meantime she would have to be alert for all possible clues.

The top shelf was still exposed. Cecilia hurried back to the bookcase and began to replace the old dusty volumes, once again covering the remaining money that was her only security in life.

The air in the sitting room was stuffy and hot. As Cecilia climbed down from the chair she felt slightly dizzy. A blackness briefly replaced her vision, and she sat suddenly on the delicate chair. The stars and the blackness finally cleared, and she took a deep breath.

A knock at the door made her jump, and instinctively she looked at her watch. Eight-ten. She had lost track of the time. Dinner must have begun already.

"Just a minute," she called, quickly picking up the chair and carrying it back to the writing table. One last hurried survey of the room assured her that everything was in place.

Composing herself, Cecilia opened the door. Then she smiled broadly with relief. Tony stood waiting on the threshold.

"Dinner's ready," he announced. "Aren't you coming?"

"It's so humid and sticky I don't think I could eat a bite," Cecilia explained. "It's very dry in Kenya, you know, and I'm not used to this weather."

Tony nodded sagely, but a hint of disappointment crossed his childish features.

"I hope you don't mind," Cecilia continued. "Please tell your father I'm sorry I didn't send word earlier that I wouldn't be dining tonight." She paused, then added, "And tell him I'll be around after dinner to give him the money for the week's tours, since your Uncle Evan is away for the evening."

"Sure," Tony agreed quickly. "You look like you could use some rest," he said seriously. "You look terrible."

Cecilia laughed in spite of her mood and watched Tony skip off down the great hallway to the dining room.

NIGHT HAD FALLEN, and still Cecilia could not bring herself to go to bed. She felt weak and uneasy, trying to sort through the tangled situation she found herself in. She knew now that she was in troubled waters way over her head. When she had gone down to the dining room just after dinner, only Catherine and Philip were present. And Catherine, her only suspect, had showed no shock at seeing Cecilia with the money. Indeed, she had gushed for some ten minutes at how splendid a "contribution" Cecilia's tours were making to the "well-being" of Chesterton.

If only she could think of some way to cut through to the truth, Cecilia agonized, she would be able to rest.

The jangle of the phone ringing on the writing table startled her. It rarely rang. Few people called to inquire about the tours as notices about them were well placed throughout Dartmouth. In any case, it was eleven-thirty at night, an odd time for someone to be calling.

"Hello," Cecilia said slowly, holding the phone tentatively at her ear.

"Evan here," came the reply. "I just returned and saw your light, then discovered your note. Would you care to discuss your proposal about the foreign tours with me now?"

It was a strange request to be making at that hour, but Cecilia thought she could detect a note of sorrow in Evan's voice. Was he lonely? Had he used her message to get her to come to him, just as she had used it in her concern over the article in the newspaper?

"Yes, that would be fine," Cecilia said, scarcely believing her own calm voice.

"In my study, then," Evan said. "I gather by the presence of your note that you'll have no trouble finding it."

"I'll be around shortly," Cecilia answered, then hung up.

For the second time that day Cecilia traced the path that led from her suite to Evan's study in the west wing. At the top of the stairs she paused. She had engineered this meeting because she had to know the truth—had Evan robbed Benningsway last night? Now, looking down the hall to her left, she saw a narrow strip of light running along the base of the massive door that marked the entrance to Evan's private domain. She suddenly realized that she had no idea just how she would discover the truth. But there was no time to attempt to devise a plan.

Cecilia tiptoed to the door of the study, not wanting to awaken the other members of the family. She knocked lightly, and the door opened instantly.

Evan took her breath away. He was formally dressed in a black tuxedo, but he had removed his bow tie, giving himself a look of casual elegance. With a sweeping motion he invited Cecilia into the softly lit room.

The study suited Evan in every respect, Cecilia thought admiringly. It was a warm and eccentric room dominated by a massive rolltop desk. The wood of the paneling, the desk and the bookcases all gleamed in the shadowy light. The leather of two great armchairs at the far end of the room had a warm well-used appearance. Only one painting hung on the wall—a tiny Impressionist piece that Cecilia couldn't identify. All around the room books and papers were neatly stacked, weighted and supported by unlikely-looking pieces of wood, stone and glass.

Cecilia felt Evan's eyes appraising her. He was looking at her as if for the first time. Nervously she smoothed her skirt. She felt that she was in some way improperly dressed compared to Evan's formal attire. She wore a sheer blue short-sleeved blouse with a tucked yoke and a print dirndl skirt with a wide waistband, and her hair fell down over her shoulders in thick waves. She wished that it were tied back neatly, as she usually wore it, but she hadn't had time to more than glance at it before setting out.

"Would you care for a brandy?" Evan said at last.

Cecilia shook her head no, then amended, "Yes, yes, thank you."

Evan smiled in amusement. "You remind me of our first meeting, Cecilia. At the train station." He walked over to the small bar that was fitted into the bookcase and poured two snifters of brandy out of a crystal decanter. "You couldn't seem to decide what to say on that occasion, either. Sweet," he said simply, handing her a brandy. "I sometimes wonder if you're not sweet sixteen instead of—what is it—nearly twenty-one?"

Cecilia felt a blush suffuse her cheeks. He was making fun of her again. "If that's the vein in which you intend to—"

"And quick," Evan interrupted. "Please sit down," he said, pointing to the two leather chairs. "I don't mean to be insulting. I've just come from a gathering of rather stuffy old people, and I find you refreshing, that's all."

"'Refreshing' is not the same as 'amusing,'" Cecilia retorted. She paused for a moment, then walked over and sat down in one of the deep leather chairs. She knew she could walk out, but she didn't want to.

"No, it's not the same," Evan agreed. "And I don't find you amusing. You must forgive me if it appears so." He sat in the other chair, then went on. "You're one of the few people I can depend on to make me smile. Perhaps I've taken advantage of the opportunity in a way that has misled you. I am not, under any circumstances, laughing at you."

Laughing with me, Cecilia thought. She had grown

up with the laughter of the men on the game preserve, survived their amusement at the way she faced each new lesson in the hardships of the wild. Her father had always said they were laughing *with* her, not *at* her, and that they respected her. Now she was having to start all over again, in England, Cecilia mused. Would her father have said that Evan was laughing with her, that he respected her, she wondered idly.

"It must be a difficult adjustment for you," Evan commented. "England is so different from Africa."

"Yes," Cecilia murmured. "The rules of the game, and the rewards, are not the same here."

"What mattered in Kenya? What rules and rewards sustained you?" Evan asked.

Cecilia was stirred by the sincerity in his voice. His tone matched the care and genuine interest that his words implied. "Courage mattered," she said reflectively, "and results. Everything was in the open—the animals, the land, our lives, our feelings. There were no hidden motives, no secret desires. We all shared a common love, a love of the preserve and all it stood for."

"How very wonderful. . ." Evan breathed.

"It was!" Cecilia returned with fervor. "It was exciting and real every minute of the day." Cecilia abruptly checked herself. It was foolish to relive the past like this. She could never make Evan—or anyone—understand. "But it's over," she finished quietly.

"I understand," Evan said softly, leaning toward her. "Your memories are all that's left to you—all that you will ever be able to keep of the past."

Cecilia felt relieved. Evan did understand! This man was reading her heart. . . .

Suddenly Cecilia sat up rigidly. What was she thinking? She had come to determine whether or not Evan was a criminal, and she had strayed far off course. She was being tricked.

Evan rose and walked around to the back of his chair, staring at her. An awkward silence hung in the air. Cecilia had to bring the conversation back to safe territory—away from her feelings, her past, and into the present.

"I gave the tour money to Philip," she said quickly.

"Yes, I know. He left it in this room. Quite a sizable sum for your first week." Strangely, Evan did not sound strained or angry. He seemed to have accepted her reticence, and Cecilia felt grateful to him. "I must compliment you," he continued. "You are giving the Chesterton tours a fine reputation already."

Cecilia looked down into the brandy snifter. The compliment, the strong scent of the liquor and the intensity of her own emotions all combined to make her feel oddly light-headed.

"I had the money changed into large bills in Dartmouth," she said quietly. "I thought . . . ."

"Very sensible," Evan finished for her. Cecilia had an inkling that he hadn't really heard her, though.

"My idea about the foreign tours came to me because of that large group of German tourists I described in the note. I think we can. . . ." Cecilia's voice trailed off. The whole conversation seemed pointless.

"I'm sure we can," Evan said, walking over to the window that opened onto the inner courtyard at the back of the manor. "I'm sure we can," he repeated.

Cecilia remained silent, trying to understand Evan's mood. What had been the real reason for his call?

"It almost frightens me," Evan said slowly, "the success of the tours. It hasn't been like this for a long time. Or maybe it only seems like a long time."

"Been like what?" Cecilia probed.

"Oh, smooth and relaxed," he answered almost dreamily. Then he turned to face back into the room. "Would you care for a cigarette?"

Cecilia shook her head. Evan took a silver box off the table between the two leather chairs, opened it and lighted a cigarette for himself. Cecilia met Evan's questioning eyes steadily, then felt rocked to the core by an intense feeling of desire, a desire bound up in the love she had tried to reject just minutes earlier.

Quickly she looked away. She was embarrassed and confused. Had Evan known what she was feeling? Cecilia couldn't tell from the tone of his voice when he next spoke.

"I guess it hasn't been so long, in the normal sense," he continued, again gazing out the open window. "I've only been back at Chesterton a little over a year. But the circumstances of my return...and my stay here...have been so taxing that perhaps I've lost track of a sense of time."

"And things were different a little over a year ago at Chesterton," Cecilia offered. She was remembering Gwen's words about the departure of the entire staff just before the girl had been hired.

"Yes, things were different," Evan confirmed, ignoring Cecilia's apparent knowledge of changes at the manor. "Emily was in love. I thought Philip was happy with his new wife. And my business was really taking off in London."

"What kind of business?" Cecilia asked. Perhaps if she could see him in some clearly enterprising light she would be able to dismiss all her fears that he might be an art thief.

"Oh, an art-investment advisory firm," Evan said off-handedly, as if his interests no longer mattered. "It was everything I wanted at the time—the culmination of my years of work at Cambridge—but now it seems so terribly unimportant."

"What's important now?" Cecilia asked gently.

"Chesterton. And not letting the success you've brought to it evaporate, as everything else seems to have since that happy time." Evan ran his fingers through his dark hair and turned to Cecilia. "Would you mind if I took off my jacket?" he asked politely.

"Of course not," Cecilia said at once.

Evan removed his jacket and rolled up the sleeves of his white silk shirt. His strong forearms glistened slightly from the heat of the night, and again Cecilia felt a sensation of desire such as she had never before experienced. She swallowed hard, then said, "Tell me about the happy times. And why they're gone."

"Maybe they're gone because they were never real," Evan said unhappily, walking over to perch on the front portion of the leather chair opposite Cecilia. "But everything *seemed* so perfect. Then everything changed. And the worst casualty was Emily. She was engaged to be married to a kind quiet man named Hillary Masterson. I really liked him. He'd built an old stable into a crack breeding farm for prized stock—Masterson Stables, he called it. Emily learned to ride like the wind there, and one day I learned that Hillary had given her his most valuable animal—Tchaikovsky—as an engagement present, instead of the traditional diamond ring.

"Then I received a letter from Philip. A shocking letter that to this day makes no sense to me. Catherine had found the strongbox containing the tour money in Hillary's car. She claimed that Hillary was after Emily's money and was stealing his way through their courtship. And she convinced Philip to accept her wild accusation. Hillary refused to defend himself and left the country before I could return."

Evan rose and walked back over to his station by the open window. When he continued his voice was low. "Emily refused to accept what had happened. She rode off into the night on Tchaikovsky, saying she would never return. But Tony found her the next day. She'd been thrown from the horse. Her right leg was smashed."

"No wonder," Cecilia breathed.

"Yes. No wonder Emily has become the unhappy bitter woman that you see today. Six months later she got up from her bed, her leg badly healed and her heart broken forever."

"And Emily is the reason you came home," Cecilia said softly.

"Emily was the reason," Evan agreed. "But Emily is only a part of why I stay. The manor, I discovered, is just as crippled as Emily. It's as if . . . as if something or someone can't bear to see us all happy. And I've got to find out—"

Suddenly Evan slammed his fist against the wall. In an instant Cecilia was on her feet and at his side. Now was the time to tell him about the stolen tour money.

Now he was prepared to bring out the stigma of Chesterton Manor. Together they would find the saboteur she knew Evan suspected.

But Cecilia didn't have a chance to speak. Evan's arms were encircling her, and she felt his mouth closing over hers. Her entire being melted into the power and magic of the kiss, and for several moments the heat of the night and their shared passion seemed to fuse their bodies. Cecilia experienced a oneness and a desire such as she had never dreamed could exist.

Slowly their bodies parted. Cecilia gazed up into Evan's face and spoke to him with her eyes, telling him that she loved him with all her heart, pleading with him to say the words that stuck in her throat. She had never said, "I love you," and she felt hopelessly unsure of her own voice.

Evan took a step back. Sadness, not love, showed in his face, and Cecilia realized suddenly that something was wrong. She opened her mouth to speak, but Evan lifted his fingers to her lips, gently silencing her. "We're...I'm not in a position to...love you, Cecilia. I can't...."

Cecilia could never remember exactly what had happened as Evan's voice trailed off. Tears had sprung instantly to her eyes, but how she'd had the courage to run from the study, she couldn't recall later.

Chapter 8

Without Tchaikovsky Cecilia would never have been able to endure the next two days. She was with him for only an hour each morning, but speeding through the orchards in the fresh dawn air, she'd found that she could transport herself to the happier times of her childhood.

The sting of Evan's rejection would never leave her, though she knew that she had succeeded in her efforts on Tony's and Emily's behalf. Soon she would be able to show them what she had achieved with Tchaikovsky. At least one part of the saboteur's plan—the beatings and the ruin of the magnificent horse—would be thwarted.

Then she would leave Chesterton. She no longer had the heart to stay on and solve the mysteries that surrounded it. Evan would have to face those puzzles without her.

Cecilia felt Tchaikovsky pull up slightly, and the

sensation jerked her from her thoughts. It had been days since the horse had resisted her direction. Then she saw why. Tony was standing under a low branch of one of the trees, munching a green apple. Cecilia drew in on the reins.

"Tony!" she exclaimed. "What are you doing up at this hour?"

"Eating green apples," Tony said, smiling. "I like them." The boy walked fearlessly up to the "monster" horse and patted him on the neck. Tchaikovsky did not stir. "Besides," Tony added, "lots of people are up."

Cecilia slipped down off Tchaikovsky's back. "Like who, for instance?" she asked warily.

"Oh," he began pensively, stroking Tchaikovsky's luxuriant mane, "like you...and me...and Catherine and Mathias."

Cecilia was alarmed. How would she get Tchaikovsky back into his stall without Mathias knowing? If he didn't know already....

Tony began to laugh when he saw Cecilia's expression. "Oh, Cecilia, I'm sorry. I shouldn't tease you. It's just that it isn't often I get to fool an adult. You don't have to worry about getting Tchaikovsky back into his stall. Mathias never gets down to the stable before ten o'clock. I should have told you that. Then you wouldn't have had to worry every morning."

"Then you knew!" Cecilia cried in wonder.

Tony nodded. "I hope you won't think I was spying on you. It's just that I like to get up early, too."

"But why didn't you tell me?" Cecilia demanded.

"Well," Tony said reflectively, "I was so happy when I saw how much Tchaikovsky liked you. I didn't want to spoil anything. I could see that you wanted it to be a secret." Tony looked thoughtfully at the half-eaten green apple, then tossed it off into the trees. "Can we have secrets together, Cecilia?"

"Looks as if we already do," Cecilia smiled.

After a moment Tony asked, "Can I tell you something—a secret?"

"Of course," Cecilia replied. "I won't tell a soul. What is it?"

"I wish Catherine—I can't call her mother, you know, because she won't allow it—anyway, I wish Catherine had never come back from London. Nobody's been happy since Catherine came back. Not even daddy."

"When did Catherine come back?"

"Oh, I don't know exactly. Sometime before summer holidays last year—Catherine was the one who said I had to leave Chesterton to go to school in Exeter. I don't really like that, either."

Cecilia could see that Tony was looking for an outlet for his well-hidden unhappiness.

"Let's walk a bit with Tchaikovsky," she said. "Would you like to hold the reins with me?"

"Oh, yes," the boy cried, reaching up to touch the leather straps attached to the bridle.

They walked through the fragrant trees in silence for a moment, then Tony said, "I don't like Mathias, either. He came back from London with Catherine, but I don't believe he knows anything about horses. Daddy said Catherine came back so she could be with him and me, but that's not true. Did you know that?"

"No, I didn't. Why did she come back if it wasn't because she missed you and your father?"

"I heard daddy telling her that there wasn't enough money for her to live in London. I'm not even sure when they got married, but I know she doesn't like Chesterton. And daddy said she could stay in London if it made her happy."

Cecilia was saddened by the depth of the troubles and confusions Tony was carrying in his young mind, but she doubted that he'd ever discussed them with anyone, not even Emily. Tony was too sensitive to Emily's unhappiness to tell her of his own. Perhaps, she thought, he had never told Evan because he felt he would somehow be disloyal to his own father—a father who, in any case, the boy was disinclined to confide in.

"She was really mad when daddy said that he would have to fire all the servants," Tony went on. "Daddy said he didn't know how it happened but that Catherine had spent so much money that he might have to sell Chesterton." Tony stopped talking suddenly and plucked another apple. He examined it for a moment, then threw it away.

"Chesterton will be yours someday, Tony," Cecilia soothed. "And don't you ever doubt it."

"Not if things keep going bad!" Tony insisted. "Chesterton is in real trouble. I know it. And when I found Emily...un...unconscious last year," he said in a choked voice, "I knew nothing would ever go...go right, again."

Suddenly Tony was sobbing. All the worry he'd been struggling with for the past year was now coming out in a flood of tears. Cecilia stopped walking and wordlessly took him into her arms. She stroked his soft red curls and held him, waiting for the boy to cry all the tears he

had been hiding. Amazingly, Tchaikovsky did not stir
when she let the reins drop.

Gradually Tony's crying slowed. He sniffed violently,
as if trying to compose himself and behave like the
imaginary adult he usually imitated. But he couldn't
quite regain his pose. He looked up into Cecilia's eyes
and moaned, "Oh, Cecilia, I don't know what's going to
happen!"

"Don't worry, Tony," Cecilia whispered. "Everything
will work out just fine."

"You won't leave, will you?" he suddenly demanded.

"Of course not," Cecilia said, wondering how she
could make such a promise when she planned to leave in
a matter of days. "Why would you even think that,
Tony?" she asked gently.

"Because Mr. Masterson left," Tony replied swiftly.

"Mr. Masterson?"

"Mr. Masterson and Aunt Emily were going to get
married. And Mr. Masterson was going to fix up our
stables—and make money with them. It would have
helped Chesterton so much! But Mr. Masterson disappeared. He was so nice. . . ."

"I promise you with all my heart that I won't leave,"
Cecilia said firmly. "Do you believe me?"

Tony nodded, and another tear escaped.

"Tony," Cecilia said brightly, "we can't let Tchaikovsky think we've forgotten him, can we? How would you
like to ride him?"

Tony's eyes opened wide. "Do you mean it?" he asked
incredulously.

"Sure. I think he's probably getting tired of just me
for a rider," Cecilia said. "Why don't you hop on with

me so that poor Tchaikovsky doesn't get bored with his morning workout?"

Tony was ecstatic, and much to Cecilia's relief the horse accepted the extra passenger with complete calm. Tony rode with her into the stables bearing the countenance of a Roman general returning in triumph.

LATER THAT DAY, Cecilia made an important discovery during the last few minutes of the afternoon's final tour. She led the visitors to the exit and smiled as each passed by mumbling various words of thanks and appreciation for an interesting tour. The gray-eyed man, as usual, was the last one in the crowd, and she reached out to touch his arm. He stopped and stared at her questioningly.

"Hillary Masterson?" she inquired softly.

"Yes," the man answered, obviously taken aback. "Who told you who I am?"

"No one," Cecilia replied. "I just guessed."

"But how could you have known I even existed?" he continued, still greatly surprised.

"That's not important at the moment," Cecilia said quickly. "But I think you and I have a great deal in common. Could we meet? Somewhere away from the manor?"

"Of course," Hillary answered more evenly. "My car is parked in the lot if you—"

"I can't leave at once," Cecilia interrupted. "Later this evening?"

"Meet me for dinner," Hillary said decisively. "Do you know the Edward III?"

It was Cecilia's turn to be uncertain. She hadn't

planned to let anyone notice her absence. She considered for a moment, then decided that since she had missed dinner once before she could do it again.

"Certainly. Eight o'clock?"

"Eight it is," confirmed Hillary, and proceeded quickly out of the manor.

The next hour and a half was a busy one for Cecilia. She began by finding Emily. With some reservation she explained that she had got a sudden urge to get away for the evening. Would anyone mind if she were not present at dinner, she asked uncertainly. Fortunately Emily was in a good mood and said that she understood perfectly that Cecilia might like an evening out. She also saved Cecilia the trouble of asking for a favor by offering the loan of her car for the evening.

Cecilia thanked her profusely, then bathed and changed her clothes. Afterward she went through the tedious procedure of checking the day's receipts against the tickets that had been issued. Everything tallied. She selected a light book off the shelf and locked it in the strongbox. Then she put the money behind the books on the top shelf of the bookcase, exactly in the spot where her own money had once rested. If the thief came around while she was gone, he or she would not be rewarded this time, she thought grimly. Regrettably, the thief would be tipped off to the fact that Cecilia expected more trouble, but it was a risk she'd decided to take. With the number of visitors the manor was receiving, she wouldn't be able to continue replacing the money indefinitely.

It was seven-forty when Emily's little car rumbled over the wooden bridge that spanned the moat, and

Cecilia was annoyed with herself for being ten minutes off schedule. She tried to concentrate on what she would say to Hillary when she got to the Edward III, but her thoughts were scattered between her conversation with Tony, her desire to tell Emily how she had trained Tchaikovsky, the beauty of the countryside in the golden evening sun—and her worries about how she would manage to stay on at Chesterton with the prospect of seeing Evan at any moment.

Valiantly Cecilia tried to keep him out of her mind entirely. Still, often she found herself speculating on his possible life of crime or his reasons for kissing her. . . . and then rejecting her. It was painful for her to dwell on the issues, for in the end she knew that what she felt for him was love, a love that would never be returned.

She managed to park and get to the Edward III by five past eight. Hillary Masterson was waiting for her outside the door.

"Hello, Mr. Masterson," she said, extending her hand, "I'm Cecilia Bennett, this summer's tour guide at Chesterton."

"I know," Hillary smiled. "I've attended one or two of those tours. Perhaps you remember me?"

Cecilia laughed. "How right you are. At this point I feel as if I know you."

"I'd like to hear more about that. Shall we go inside?"

Cecilia agreed, and as soon as they were inside the door a hostess approached them. To Cecilia's surprise, what she had thought was merely a pub was really a very nice restaurant. The upper floor had been furnished in a rustic nautical style, and the menu was extensive.

Not knowing quite where to begin, she and Hillary studied the menu over predinner drinks. Hillary finally chose a mixed grill with fried potatoes while Cecilia decided on broiled lemon sole and fresh asparagus with hollandaise sauce. When the waitress had left, Cecilia found the words to begin the important conversation.

"I said that I thought you and I had a lot in common," she said slowly. "I think that we've both been framed by the same Cedric-Browne—and that we both have a certain affection for different Cedric-Brownes."

Hillary raised an eyebrow, then said quietly, "I presume that you mean Catherine has taken the tour money again and that you and Emily have developed a friendship?"

Cecilia was taken aback by his directness. She took a sip of cool white wine and stared back at Hillary. His soft voice and sandy hair were a startling contrast to his words. More than ever she doubted that he was a thief.

"I don't know," Cecilia said at last. "Or rather, I know that I care for Emily. But I don't know that Catherine took the tour money, though you're right about it having been stolen."

Hillary shook his head sadly. "I should never have left England. It was wrong of me to leave Emily alone at Chesterton when I knew that something terrible was happening. But I didn't know...I didn't know...."

"Didn't know what?" Cecilia asked calmly.

"I didn't know, and I still don't know what Emily thought...what she felt when Philip and Catherine accused me." Cecilia remained silent, and Hillary raised his penetrating gray eyes to fix them on Cecilia. "Do you know? Did she tell you about me?"

"No," she answered, wishing she did know how Emily felt. "I learned of your circumstances from Evan and Tony. But you haven't shown much faith in Emily by questioning her loyalty, have you?" Cecilia was on shaky ground now, for she knew that her words implied a belief that Emily still loved Hillary. She prayed her guess was accurate.

"You're right, of course," Hillary said quickly. "But everything happened so fast. And it was all so unreasonable. The damn strongbox in my car, Catherine's accusation, then Philip's forbidding me to see his sister—Emily was nowhere to be found and I flew into a kind of panic. I left Masterson Stables the very night it happened; I couldn't bear the thought that my integrity had been questioned by the Cedric-Brownes. I spent the entire summer in Scotland at my brother's farm. And since I've been back no one has said a word to me about Chesterton. It's as if the whole country has conspired to put a wall between Chesterton and me."

Hillary drank deeply from the tall glass of dark stout he had ordered, but the brew couldn't remove the anguished look from his face. "Finally I couldn't stay away any longer. I started coming to your tours, just to be at Chesterton...and hoping to get a glimpse of Emily. But I haven't. I've spent the past winter trying to sort out what's happened; all I know is that I want to see Emily."

Cecilia was horrified when she realized what Hillary was saying. He didn't know about Emily's accident on Tchaikovsky.... It hardly seemed possible.

"So you've neither seen nor heard anything of Emily for the past year?"

Hillary shook his head. "No, I haven't," he sighed. A multitude of thoughts rushed through Cecilia's head. Should she tell Hillary about the accident—and about Emily's present state of mind? What would it accomplish if she did? Hillary was already distressed enough as it was. And Emily had never confided in her. Cecilia felt she had to respect certain limits in acting as a go-between for the pair. At least it was comforting to know that Hillary had stayed away not knowing how much Emily needed him.

At last she spoke. "Well, I don't think you've given things a proper chance. I can't tell you how Emily feels about you today, but I can tell you that she's very unhappy. Chesterton isn't a very pleasant place these days."

The waitress arrived with their meals, and for a few minutes Hillary and Cecilia ate in silence. Theirs was not really a conversation designed to stimulate the appetite, despite the high quality of the food. Soon they stopped eating.

"Why did you approach me?" Hillary asked. "You're obviously a clever person to have figured out who I am. You must have something in mind."

"I thought that together we might be able to set matters straight at Chesterton," Cecilia replied. "And I thought that you must still have some feelings for Emily. Otherwise you wouldn't be spending your time coming to my repetitious tours just so you could be close to her."

Hillary smiled his unique, sad, thin smile. "I love Emily. Nothing will ever change that."

Cecilia wanted to shout, "And Emily loves you, too!"

but she couldn't. Not just yet. Instead she said, "You suspect Catherine?"

Hillary made an offhanded gesture. "Oh, yes, I suspect Catherine. But I have no evidence. To me Catherine just never seemed to fit."

"At Chesterton?"

"At all. She was always so smooth, but I could never find anything genuine about her. And I could never figure out why she married Philip. Perhaps it was her background that made me suspicious."

Cecilia became alert. Hillary's estimation of Catherine was almost identical with her own—suspicion without cause. "What is her background? I've never heard a word about it."

"Catherine was a stage actress before she married Philip. Small-time, I understand. You probably never heard anything about it because Emily once accused her of acting her way through every moment at Chesterton just so that she could keep Philip—and his money. Philip was furious. He insisted that Catherine's profession never again be mentioned and that Tony should never know the truth. A touch of old-fashioned prudery, I thought at the time, but I guess Emily has honored his wishes."

The information hit Cecilia with the force of a hammer. Perhaps she had seen Catherine's picture on an old poster in London and that was why she'd recognized her, she reasoned. In any case, it might explain why Catherine had managed to appear so poised when she'd produced the tour money the other night after it had been stolen. If Catherine were indeed the thief....

"We've got to find out if Catherine is behind all this,"

Cecilia said urgently. "After all, someone is trying to destroy Chesterton—and you don't know the extent of it. It's not Evan and it's not Emily, and Philip doesn't have enough spirit to try it, even if he does have a motive."

"I've always liked Evan," Hillary said reflectively. "I thought once about approaching him, but then I thought that if Emily didn't really love me...well, it would just make matters worse. Philip used to be different, too, you know."

"No, I didn't know," Cecilia said. She was gratified to hear that Hillary liked Evan—despite her own disappointments in him—and she was interested in the fact that Philip had changed in some way. But Hillary was straying from the point.

"Yes," Hillary mused. "I've known Philip since I was a child. He was a lot like Evan as a boy. Decisive, quick, sure of himself. He was never as bright as Evan, mind you, but he was a nice fellow. When the elder Cedric-Brownes were killed in a plane crash it was Philip's young wife who really took over and ran Chesterton. She was both kind and intelligent. Unfortunately she died giving birth to Tony, and Philip has never really known any happiness since or had much sense of conviction, even where the boy is concerned."

Cecilia leaned back in the comfortable captain's chair. Hillary was lost in his memories. She sipped her wine and thought for a moment. It all made sense now. Evan had probably tried to contact Hillary when he'd returned to Chesterton after Emily's accident, but Hillary would have been in Scotland by then. She doubted that anyone at Masterson Stables would have revealed

Hillary's whereabouts to a Cedric-Browne. She still didn't understand though, what Catherine's motive could be, but the circumstantial evidence was mounting. Cecilia had to get Hillary back to the present so that they could plan a course of action.

"Hillary," she said gently, "we can't let Catherine—if it is Catherine—get away with this. She's already stolen a year from you and Emily, and she may be trying to steal Chesterton from little Tony, though how, I don't know."

Hillary's gray eyes met Cecilia's, and he nodded gravely. "You're right, of course, but I don't see what we can do now. You must have received the blame for stealing the tour money and been asked to leave. I don't think your word and mine would count very much with Philip at this point."

Cecilia leaned forward excitedly. "But I didn't tell anyone the money was stolen. I replaced the stolen money myself. Only the thief knows that."

"Cecilia, you've taken a terrible risk!" For the first time Hillary became animated.

"Sometimes taking risks is the only way you can get something. And we're going to have to take a few more before this is over," Cecilia assured him. "We've got to let the thief believe that he or she has succeeded and that the money will keep coming while the thefts go unrevealed." Cecilia stared at Hillary earnestly. "Then we've got to drop the net. But it won't work without your help, Hillary. We've got to move fast."

Hillary did not hesitate. He had been convinced. He listened in awe as Cecilia sketched out the details of her plan, and he agreed to play his part.

Driving back to Chesterton, Cecilia felt both exhilarated and frightened. Her concentration was intense as she reviewed each aspect of the plan she and Hillary had agreed upon. Even Hillary's revelations about the Cedric-Browne family didn't deter her from going ahead with their scheme.

As Cecilia guided Emily's little car across the bridge spanning the moat around Chesterton, she was certain that she saw a shadow among the trees. She thought it might be Mathias, but she couldn't be certain. Still, Mathias kept odd hours, and Cecilia guessed he was on his way to or from a rendezvous with Catherine.

Chapter 9

It was almost noon, and Cecilia was in the midst of conducting a tour when a scream suddenly sliced through her words. The shriek elongated into an anguished wail, and Cecilia knew at once that Tony needed her.

Instinctively she began to move toward the sound of distress. A wall of dumbstruck bodies blocked her way. She'd forgotten momentarily that she was addressing a group of tourists, tourists whose puzzled faces reflected a multitude of questions.

Cancel the tour, Cecilia thought. But as soon as the thought was formed the scream began to fade. Tony must be running to the west wing. If Tony could run, Cecilia assumed he would find help from Emily—or Gwen, if Emily were away teaching. And if she canceled the tour instead of calming the visitors, it would only give Chesterton an unsavory reputation.

She glanced at her watch. In ten minutes this last tour of the morning would be completed.

"That, ladies and gentlemen, was the voice of the next earl of Chesterton, Anthony Cedric-Browne." She managed a smile and saw that most of the faces before her showed surprise rather than real concern. "He's all of eleven years old, and as I'm sure most of you know, tragedies take on a special definition to a little boy." Several people nodded in agreement. Cecilia sighed in relief. She had succeeded in making them relax.

"Now, if you'd like to follow me we'll have a look at the gallery, a room of rich tradition in the Cedric-Browne family."

The herd followed Cecilia unquestioningly, and with little difficulty she brought them back into the wonderstruck state in which most tourists proceeded through the east wing. Cecilia wouldn't have imagined herself capable of exercising so much self-control, but she was able to bid the group goodbye in ten minutes, showing complete outward calm.

Inside, however, her heart beat at a wild pace. Tony would let out such a cry only in the fact of true disaster. Something more terrible than she could even guess had happened. And scarcely before the last visitor was out the door she ran from the gallery to the dining room, where the family would by now certainly be assembled.

As she entered the salon Cecilia could once again hear Tony's choked sobs. Without pause she rushed into the dining room. The scene that greeted her was shocking.

A sumptuous array of cold shellfish had already been laid out on the table. Tony was buried in Emily's arms, crying now that he had exhausted his lungs by screaming. Philip was standing with his back to the scene, staring out the window at the far end of the room while Catherine was helping herself to a boiled shrimp. Evan was absent.

"What happened?" Cecilia demanded.

Tony looked up at the sound of her voice. "Oh, Cecilia, it was so awful!" he wailed anew. "Blood was everywhere. The cows. . . ." Fresh sobs made it impossible for the boy to continue.

"Two of our prized Jersey cows have been butchered," Emily explained in a monotone. "Tony came across them in the meadow."

Cecilia gasped. "Do you mean—"

"I don't think we'll achieve anything by reviewing the details," Philip cut in. "Particularly as we stand here before our noonday meal."

How could Philip think about lunch when his son had barely recovered from hysteria, Cecilia thought, shocked.

"That's quite enough!" Catherine proclaimed. "Now you, young man, will sit down and behave like the heir to Chesterton Manor. Two beasts are not two people. And we'll discuss this like the family we are. Several of the dairy men are already attending to the, uh, matter. It is for us to decide upon its significance."

In a daze, Cecilia moved to her place. She felt vaguely nauseated by the sight of food. The sabotage had reached a new and horrific low. And she had thought she could stop it. . . .

"You've got to initiate a full-scale investigation at once," Emily said sternly to her brother.

Philip swayed back and forth in his chair, as if moving his shoulders from side to side would help him find a reply. Cecilia wished Evan were present.

"I don't think the mishaps at Chesterton Manor need

be made public," Catherine said calmly. "Did you get some lobster, Philip, darling?"

Philip nodded, then shrugged and took the platter Catherine was extending to him.

"Mishaps!" Emily exclaimed. "Two beautiful animals—murdered. There's no other word for it, Catherine. 'Mishaps' indeed!"

"I don't believe the term 'murder' can properly be applied to cows, Emily," Catherine interjected.

"All right, Catherine, we'll play it your way," Emily said leveling her eyes at her sister-in-law. "Those two cows were a valuable asset to Chesterton—'asset' as in 'money,'" she stressed. "I won't bore you with the particulars of dairying—I know how base you find it—but the quality of the stock determines the prestige of the dairy. And Mirabel and Winnifred have had priceless pedigrees. You can't replace—"

"I never said anything about replacing them," Catherine protested innocently. "Did you decorate these *oeufs en gelée*, Emily? They're lovely, truly lovely."

Emily glared at her brother, then back at Catherine. The contrast between each of the family members was so great that Cecilia found it hard to remain seated. She was sickened by the news of the slaughter, but she found that Catherine's nonchalance, in its own way, was even more revolting. As for the placid way in which Philip was plowing through his rich meal, she felt she understood that. He ate to avoid conflict and the responsibility and force of character in a household that constantly demanded all three.

Catherine sighed and put her fork down. "All right, Emily, we will approach this in *your* way. I would have

hoped that we could avoid any further histrionics and enjoy our lunch, but obviously you find that impossible."

Emily took a sip of white wine from the crystal goblet
at her right and managed to wait for Catherine to continue.

"As I was saying earlier," Catherine went on, "I think a
formal investigation—with the attendant publicity—will
only serve to diminish the value of the estate. Oh, rumors
are inevitable, but once the police are involved the value
is certain to be jeopardized."

"Diminish the value?" Emily repeated in wonder.
"What are you talking about? The value has already been
diminished by the loss of these two fine animals and by
countless other disasters. The only way to preserve the
'value of the estate' is to solve the crime that took place
here this morning," she argued.

"I really must differ with you, dear," Catherine said
patronizingly. "But then, your title to Chesterton is in
name only. You see, I'm thinking of Tony's welfare as I
speak."

At the sound of his name Tony looked up. The shift in
everyone's attention had calmed him, and for the past
several minutes he had been staring absently at his plate.
It hurt Cecilia to watch him, for she knew that he had re-
treated into his own familiar world of solitary sorrow, a
world that he had shared briefly with her in the orchard.

"You wouldn't want to endanger Tony's inheritance,
now would you?" Catherine inquired reasonably.

The question clearly baffled Emily. Philip, too, was
surprised enough by the tack his wife was taking to stop
eating for a moment. Obviously Tony's well-being was
not one of Catherine's usual concerns.

"Of course I don't want to endanger Tony's inheritance," Emily agreed grudgingly. "But I don't see how lying about what's happened here today is in any way beneficial to Tony."

Unexpectedly Philip spoke. "I'd like to do the best I can for Tony," he said quietly, "but I just don't know what's best...."

"Oh, this is ridiculous!" Emily cried in exasperation. "What's best is to get to the bottom of all this *deliberate* destruction, Philip! This morning's attacks are only the latest in a well-established pattern of disasters. Not another apple tree for miles around has been afflicted with disease—only Chesterton's trees have! No one else seems to have trouble keeping their milking machines running smoothly—the same type with which we have endless difficulty. And just a few years ago none of us would have thought twice about getting the stables painted. Now it's a major expenditure to be deferred as long as possible. Wake up, Philip!" Emily shouted, but she was staring directly at her brother's wife.

"I think you've listed the difficulties—"

"Oh, shut up, Catherine," Emily snapped. "What do you know? You won't even give up a few of your luxuries so that the barn roof can be properly repaired! Patches! The barn needs more than—"

"Please, Emily," Philip interrupted sadly. "It's not going to help to get overexcited. We've simply got to approach these difficulties as best we can. We'll pull through." Philip, however, showed no sign of believing this statement.

"I think Emily's right," Catherine said forcefully with a toss of her shimmering blond hair.

Cecilia watched Emily's brown eyes flash with confusion, then she saw the woman's surprise quickly being replaced by suspicion.

"Exactly what are you saying?" Emily asked slowly.

"That Chesterton is floundering," Catherine rejoined smartly, "just as you have so rightly pointed out." She paused for a moment to cut a stalk of heart of palm, then continued more calmly. "The time for sale has come."

"Sale!" Emily and Tony shouted in unison.

"Why, of course." Catherine's tone was impassive. She raised the small dove-white slice of heart of palm to her lips, then quickly surveyed each of the faces at the table.

"Darling," Philip said uneasily, "I don't really feel free to, uh, sell...Chesterton."

"But darling," Catherine gushed in reply, "the manor is yours—and Tony's, naturally. Your responsibility is to safeguard your inheritance and the honor of the Cedric-Browne name. It would hardly do for you to be remembered as 'Philip, the eleventh earl of Chesterton under whom the manor fell into ruin,' now, would it? Better that you should make a positive decision to let this relic pass from the family and live your life in the style your title affords, dear.

"And obviously, my suggestion that we keep this morning's incident to ourselves is based on my desire to have you and little Tony realize the maximum benefit from the sale. It wouldn't do for us to frighten prospective buyers at this point."

"Sell Chesterton..." was all Philip could manage to say.

"Philip!" Emily shouted. "Show some backbone!

Catherine is trying to make you destroy everything you were raised to honor."

"That's a nasty thing to say, Emily," her sister-in-law interjected. "You're upset over the cows, but you *know* I wouldn't do anything to hurt Chesterton."

"I don't know anything of the kind. But I do know that your talents as an actress are—"

"Not now, Emily!" Philip boomed.

Philip's unexpected outburst was like a thunderclap. For several minutes no one spoke.

Cecilia was mystified by Philip's sudden show of spirit. He had sat all but mute throughout the discussion of Chesterton's future, yet he had asserted himself to protect Catherine. Somehow, Cecilia thought, he must feel helpless to stop the destruction of Chesterton but strong enough to hold on to his pretty young wife. Or perhaps the loss of the manor was something he privately had come to accept. The loss of a second wife, however, would be too much for him.

Catherine recovered first. "I will take it upon myself to consult a real-estate agent first thing—"

"You can't take away Chesterton!" Tony suddenly screamed. "It's my home!" Tony jumped up from his chair apparently dizzy from the tremendous strain he'd been under since discovering the dead cows. His soft face distorted into a grimace of terrible pain. "I hate you, Catherine!" he bellowed, as he ran from the room.

Emily rose. "You will make no decisions about Chesterton Manor until you have had a chance to discuss them with Evan, Philip," she said tonelessly. "Now, I'm going to try to calm *your* son." Emily limped from the dining room on these last words.

Philip, Catherine and Cecilia sat in silence for a while. Cecilia had barely said a word since she'd entered the room. Now she half-expected to be asked to leave. But she would wait until Philip or Catherine took that step. She had to hear all she could of what Catherine was trying to engineer. And she wanted to know Philip's decision.

"Emily's right," Philip said at last. "I can't do anything until I have a chance to talk with Evan. I'll have to make a report to the police, and when Evan—"

"Why don't you just bring everything to a halt at the manor until you have a chance to see Evan, Philip dear?" Catherine trained her blue eyes on her husband, and Cecilia thought she saw Catherine willing her eyes to look warm and adoring. To Cecilia the eyes had all the affection of a piece of cheaply colored glass.

"I think it's only reasonable, after what has happened to the animals," Catherine went on, "for you to call a moratorium on all operations at Chesterton. Including the tours," she said, looking for the first time at Cecilia.

Philip's brow furrowed slightly. The plumpness of his face prevented him from ever showing much facial expression, but now he was clearly torn between his wife's wishes and his own conscience.

"Well, Catherine, I just don't know," he began. "I hate to ask Cecilia to carry on after what's happened—I don't want to put her in any danger."

"I know you don't, Philip," Catherine said easily. "That's why the tours should be stopped while we plan for the sale."

"Sale..." Philip said shakily. Then he seemed to become aware of Cecilia's presence. "I'm sorry you had to hear all this, Cecilia. I guess that wasn't very polite. Maybe you'd be more comfortable if we did stop the tours until some decision is made. . . ."

Cecilia's mind was whirring. If Catherine had her way all that she and Hillary had planned would have to abandoned. And if Catherine wanted the tours stopped there had to be a reason why; there had to be something sinister in the wings. Cecilia would somehow have to convince Philip to let her continue with the tours—and her plan—without sounding too eager.

"I was hired to do a job here," Cecilia began slowly, "and I don't like the idea of my not following through on an agreement. I'm not afraid to continue, and if you'll forgive my forwardness, I don't think it would do the reputation of Chesterton Manor any good to have this morning's news bandied about with the news that the tours have been canceled. You can't possibly hope for total secrecy."

"Oh, well, that's a good point," Philip conceded off-handedly.

"But, Cecilia, dear," Catherine crooned, "you mustn't let your sense of professional duty get in the way of your own sanity. I don't think it's fair for us to ask you to continue working under the circumstances. Think of the questions you might have to fend off once the news of the slaughter gets out."

"I'm sure I can handle that just as gracefully as I did the wrenching sound of Tony's scream this morning," Cecilia replied.

"There's also the matter of the money from the tours," Catherine said casually. "Whoever slaughtered the cows might try to steal the money. It's kept in your room, is it not?"

"How right you are, Catherine," said Cecilia. Then she turned to face Philip. "If his Lordship would consent to having me turn over the money at dinner each evening, then there will be no need for any of us to be concerned about theft. Furthermore, I will be pleased to continue offering the tours for as long as his Lordship desires."

"That's very kind of you," Philip said absently. "Perhaps that's best, don't you think, Catherine? Until we get everything straightened out."

Catherine made no reply, and Cecilia rose.

"I'm sure that the crowd for the two-o'clock tour has already gathered just beyond the bridge," Cecilia said, consulting her watch. "If you'd like me to carry on, I had best excuse myself."

Philip made a vague gesture toward the door. "Yes, yes, thank you, Cecilia," he said. "I deeply appreciate your sense of responsibility and devotion to the manor."

CECILIA SLIPPED BETWEEN THE COOL SHEETS of her bed, relieved that the day was at last over. She was still deeply troubled by the news of the brutal slaying of the cows and even more troubled by the impact the incident was having on Tony. Yet as she looked back over the day she couldn't help but feel a sense of progress: she felt certain that she now understood Catherine quite well.

The afternoon had been a particularly difficult one. News of the brutal killing of two valuable Jersey cows had spread quickly. Cecilia hadn't expected that the tourists who visited the manor would know of the disaster so soon. Yet in each afternoon tour she had been forced to try to come up with a few words of explanation. It hadn't been easy, given that there were no suspects whom she could name openly. Furthermore, Philip had not even called in the police, so she couldn't dismiss the matter simply by saying that the incident was under official investigation.

The strain had made her feel especially edgy as the afternoon wore on. Several times when she had gone out to greet the visitors at the wooden bridge she'd imagined that it was creaking in a new and ominous way. But she had told herself sternly that her nerves were getting the better of her and that the bridge was not groaning under the weight of the tourists. How could it be? Cars passed over it every day.

After the last tour she had checked the day's receipts. Then she had left the money, her accounting books and the unlocked strongbox out on the writing table, as if matters had suddenly taken her away from her task. When she returned from a long and refreshing walk the money was gone.

Pleased that the plan was working so far, Cecilia had gone downstairs to dinner with a hearty appetite. She'd been disappointed to learn that Emily had taken Tony into Dartmouth for the evening and that Evan had not yet returned from wherever he had been for the past two days. But she was gratified to see a flicker of surprise cross Catherine's face when she presented the tour money—her own money—to Philip. Catherine must have expected something entirely different, Cecilia thought with grim satisfaction.

The dinner conversation was almost nonexistent. Catherine made a few comments about the importance of selling Chesterton quickly, but Philip was quiet and distant. He appeared to be more troubled than Cecilia had ever seen him, caught as he was between warring loyalties and hampered by his own inadequacies, conscience and simply indecision.

Cecilia turned in bed, savoring the satisfaction she felt in having learned so much in one day. Now she could assign a motive to Catherine. The beautiful former actress was not interested nearly as much in the title her husband possessed or the prestige that Chesterton conferred as she was in money—money with which she could lead an extravagant life in London, presumably with Mathias.

So, Cecilia reasoned, Catherine had a double motive for stealing the tour money. On the one hand, she had hoped to drive Cecilia away, adding yet one more disaster to the case she was building so that she could lobby for the sale of Chesterton. And on the other hand, a thousand dollars here and there could be useful to Catherine, whose rich tastes had already bled a fair portion of the Cedric-Browne fortune.

As for the sickening boldness of some of Catherine's attacks on the manor, it was not difficult for Cecilia to imagine Mathias carrying out the deeds. She was certain that Mathias possessed the cruelty to beat Tchaikovsky. Cecilia could easily picture him killing the poor cows. But Mathias would have been conspicuous inside the manor itself, so Catherine had probably been the one to take the tour money. Soon, Cecilia told herself comfortingly, she and Hillary would expose Catherine's greed.

Chapter 10

There was a little skip in Cecilia's step as she crossed the drive to receive another group of tourists. She had been able to keep the tours going—in fact, she'd even had to send people away—despite the rumors about Chesterton that were circulating in Dartmouth. It had occurred to her that people might be coming because of the gossip, but she'd soon dismissed the idea. After that first afternoon few people had even asked about the killing of the cows. Clearly the townspeople had been able to separate their feelings about the manor from their assessment of the tours' quality. And they were continuing to send visitors by the score.

Cecilia's spirits had lifted considerably when Evan had returned the day after the cows had been slaughtered. As usual, there had been no explanation for his absence, but that no longer worried her. Without any real evidence, she felt that she had got her answer that night in the study. She was now completely convinced that Evan wasn't involved in the Dartmouth crime wave. Though there were aspects of his behavior she still couldn't explain, she fully believed that his integrity was beyond question. She was sure that his motives for being at Chesterton were totally unselfish.

Immediately upon his return Evan had taken charge of the divided family, convincing Philip that the manor could not be sold and silencing Catherine. He had reported the slaughter of the cows to the police without hesitation. But most of all, Cecilia would never forget the kind and tender way he had thanked her for carrying on with her job, thereby saving the reputation of the Chesterton tours. She knew that his thanks had been genuine and his respect complete. Cecilia hadn't even reproached herself for feeling honored by his attention. True, his words had not been motivated by love, but the respect and thanks of a man such as Evan Cedric-Browne were something she would cherish long after she left Chesterton. Whoever she was, the woman who was dear to him was very lucky indeed, Cecilia thought miserably. Evan's strange rebuff of her own love for him had thoroughly dashed any hopes she'd entertained that he wasn't involved with another woman.

Cecilia paused at the edge of the bridge and gazed down at the steep sides of the moat into the deep water. Today the water was a beautiful crystal blue, perfectly reflecting her image in the afternoon sun. Her dark hair was tied back in a low ponytail, and she wore a simple white dress with a scoop neck. Excitement had brought a blush to her cheeks: today was the day she had been waiting for. . . .

Hearing voices, Cecilia glanced toward the wooded

path that led in from the tourists' parking lot. A large crowd was approaching, perhaps as many as thirty tourists, she judged. Cecilia knew she couldn't lead that many people through the manor at one time, but there was one person she would not turn away: Hillary Masterson. Today was the day she and Hillary would expose the thief, and by tonight Chesterton would begin a new era.

Nothing could go wrong, Cecilia thought confidently. Catherine—if it was Catherine—had played into their hands perfectly. Each night since the slaughter of the cows Cecilia had found another way to make the money for the day's tours accessible to the thief. Each night the thief had taken the bait. The pattern set, she and Hillary had decided that there was no longer any room for failure. The scene was certain to be reenacted. But this time Hillary would have an opportunity to find Evan and Philip. The three men would be hiding in her bedroom when the thief came into the sitting room to make the now easy collection.

Swelled by her excitement, Cecilia stepped onto the bridge and waited for the group to collect so that she could make her formal welcome. The sound of leather sandals and heavy walking shoes falling on the wooden beams of the bridge mixed with the clatter of happy expectant voices. A tight cluster of people formed. The old wooden bridge groaned. Suddenly it began to give way. Utter bedlam followed.

Cecilia felt herself sliding as she heard the terrible crunching noise of the great beams of wood, and the next thing she knew, the bridge was collapsing. A little girl's scream rose up. Instantly the frightened cries of thirty people filled the air. The shouts and crashing intensified. Cecilia was gripped with real terror—for herself and for those for whom she was responsible.

The first helpless bodies splashed down into the water. The screams reached a fever pitch. Cecilia continued to slide down toward the vortex of smashed wood at the bridge's center. She felt a hand on her skirt, then a sharp pain in her ankle. Desperately she reached for the hand tugging at her skirt while trying to grasp a small shrub on the manor side of the moat. She caught a branch and pulled herself free from the collapsing bridge. The sound of fabric's ripping came to her ears through the awful din. She looked down at her skirt just in time to see a terrified child, no older than six, slipping down the steep side of the moat. Her head banged ominously as she fell. Helplessly Cecilia watched the little girl hit the water.

In a flash, a man who'd managed to get off the ruined bridge dove in after the child. For several seconds Cecilia could not pick out the face of the child in the water. Then the diver came up. In his arms was the little girl, unconscious.

Cecilia could hardly believe her eyes. Twelve feet below her was a scene of unspeakable chaos, an absolute riot of terror and confusion. The lovely blue water was filled with thrashing arms and legs, screaming people, floating cameras and possessions. Here and there a good swimmer held a flailing and hysterical child in his arms.

Scrambling to her feet, Cecilia felt a sharp stab. A shaving from one of the beams was lodged in her ankle. Closing her eyes, Cecilia pulled the thick splinter free.

She nearly fell backward. She took a deep breath, trying to stave off the dizziness of intense pain and fear. Then the screams penetrated her mind again. She had to get help.

She began a staggering run across the drive, but a hand reached out to stop her. "Cecilia!" Tony cried. "You're hurt!" The boy was carrying a long length of rope, which he dropped when he reached out to Cecilia. The pair bent simultaneously to retrieve the rope and their bodies clunked together.

"Let me get it, Cecilia," gasped Tony.

"More help," Cecilia panted. "Get more help...."

"It's all right," Tony said, grabbing her hand. "Emily's calling the fire department and the police. Evan's on his way, too." As he spoke the young boy nearly dragged Cecilia back to the devastation at the bridge.

"Tony, thank God," Cecilia managed. "All those people—"

"I know, I know," Tony interrupted. "Here, take this," he ordered, tossing her the end of the rope.

Tony's clear mind helped Cecilia to pull herself back together. She had been so lost in her thoughts about the success the day would bring.... The day's success! Hillary had to be somewhere in the crowd, Cecilia thought anxiously. Was he trapped in the moat?

Taking her eyes off the person reaching for the other end of the rope, she scanned the faces below her. But Hillary was nowhere to be seen. Cecilia looked across the bridge. Half a dozen people had managed to escape falling into the water. Then she sighted him. Hillary was among the small group. She could see his sandy blond hair as he bent over an elderly lady whom he'd appar-

ently pulled to safety. Hillary's head jerked up briefly;
he seemed to be looking at a spot beyond Cecilia.
Quickly he pulled another person to the old woman's
side. Then he broke into a run away from the bridge and
into the trees.

Cecilia whirled to see what had triggered Hillary's
reaction. She didn't have far to look. The sudden sensation of Evan's arms closing around her provided the
answer.

"Oh, my Cecilia," she heard him saying. "You're
hurt. You can't be trying to. . . ."

Cecilia felt his strong arms sweep her up. Her legs fell
limp as he supported her under her knees, but she
couldn't discern what he was saying over the roar of the
screams. He set her down finally, but the sun beat into
her eyes and eventually she closed them, feeling consciousness slip away.

TENTATIVELY CECILIA STEPPED OUT OF BED. She gradually
increased the amount of weight on her injured ankle and
was relieved that the pain was minimal. A thick white
bandage made it difficult for her to bend the joint, but
she found that she could walk without too much difficulty.

Slowly she made her way to the window and pulled
the blind. The sun still shone brightly, and she checked
her watch. She had slept for two hours. Perhaps Evan
had been right to insist that the doctor give her something to calm her nerves and help her sleep. She no
longer felt upset, just sad.

She tried to piece together what had happened after
Evan had set her down, away from the flurry of activity

at the bridge. She'd heard the noisy approach of the fire department, and then she had propped herself up on one elbow to watch the firefighters rescue the people floundering in the water. Their equipment had made this look like a simple procedure. There had been several policemen, too. One had come over and asked her a few questions, but she couldn't remember what she'd answered. There was little that she could say without throwing wild accusations at Catherine and Mathias. And she had no evidence.

Cecilia walked carefully into the sitting room, staring through the window at the scene of the disaster. No one was near the bridge now. She guessed that the doctor had been among the last to leave.

Five people had been taken to the hospital. Three of these had been injured by the ragged beams of the bridge as they fell or scrambled to safety, as had Cecilia. One was the little girl whom Cecilia had failed to save. Artificial respiration had revived her, but her parents had rightfully insisted that she be given a thorough examination. The last person to go to the hospital had been a Frenchman whose command of English was slight. Apparently he had lost his only pair of contact lenses when he hit the water and had become hysterical at the prospect of being stranded in Dartmouth without them.

Lastly the doctor had attended to Cecilia. Her ankle had required several stitches, and she had been given a tetanus shot. She remembered Evan standing close by as the doctor put on the bandage.

Evan.... Had he really said, "Oh, my Cecilia," or was the memory nothing more than a wish? Could he really care for her? The words "*my* Cecilia" echoed in her mind.

But it didn't matter, not now. At the moment Cecilia could think clearly on only one point: what had happened this afternoon was that she and Hillary had failed. And they had no plan to fall back on. With the tours stopped, they had no bait with which to lure the thief. There was nothing they could do now to expose this one aspect of the sabotage that had been inflicted upon the manor. Hope was gone.

Suddenly Cecilia sank down into the armchair. Her mind must still be full of fog, she thought wonderingly. She was missing something vitally important—more important than everything that had happened so far. This afternoon was more than just a disaster that had greatly inconvenienced a small group of tourists and spelled the end of the Chesterton tours. This afternoon was a sign, a sign of something that she should have suspected long before now. . . .

Catherine and Mathias would stop at nothing, Cecilia realized. This afternoon they had risked human lives. The sabotage of the bridge could have resulted in several deaths. Any delay in exposing those two ruthless schemers might bring others into ultimate danger, Cecilia thought with a jolt. Perhaps Catherine had tried to stop the tours so that the victim of the collapsed bridge would be a Cedric-Browne—a specific member of the family or even more than one. Cecilia couldn't think of a single person whom Catherine would hesitate to eliminate.

There was only one thing left for her to do, Cecilia decided. She had to take Evan into her confidence. After dinner she would ask to see him alone. Then she would reveal everything she and Hillary suspected. She would tell him about the stolen tour money. She had been foolish to let the way Evan had treated her in his study cloud her mind in the first place. She had known for days that the situation was much more serious than she'd wanted to believe. Now, more than ever, she needed Evan's help.

Easing her way into the bedroom, Cecilia thought fleetingly that it would be nice to take a bath. But her bandaged ankle made the proposition awkward, and she decided it was more important for her to find Evan. Reaching into her closet, she pulled out the first thing that her hand touched. It was the blue printed dirndl skirt she'd worn the night she had met with Evan in his study. . . .

Well, so what, she thought unhappily. She didn't care what memories were attached to the skirt. She pulled a white knitted top over her head and glanced at herself in the mirror. No amount of makeup or lipstick could hide the strain in her face, she told herself, deciding to skip it.

She gathered up what tour money there was and put it in a large brown envelope. The last installment. It gave her no pleasure to think that for the first time she would actually be turning over the real tour money. She checked her watch again. It was nearly eight o'clock; time to go.

The great central hallway seemed longer than usual as Cecilia made her way slowly to the west wing. But she knew that her tremendous sense of defeat and not her injured ankle made it seem long. She was surprised to hear voices coming from the salon. It was very unlike the family to gather except for a meal, and then they always met in the dining room. Cecilia wondered if the bridge disaster was sufficient cause to bring them together so early. But she was in no mood to eavesdrop. With little satisfaction, she felt that the Cedric-Browne family now had no secrets from her.

"I was going to come down and help you!" Tony cried the minute he saw Cecilia approach. "You shouldn't have walked down here without someone to take your arm." The small boy was quickly at her side, and Cecilia smiled appreciatively as he guided her to a comfortable chair.

"How are you feeling?" Emily and Catherine chorused, with Philip joining in somewhat belatedly to ask the same question.

"Fine," Cecilia sighed, knowing that the lie must be obvious. "My ankle hardly hurts at all." At least that much was true. She could hardly share with the whole group the deep sorrow she felt at the way her plan had been thwarted.

"No matter what my feelings are about what has happened, I wouldn't want you to suffer injury." This odd remark came from Evan.

"What are you talking about?" Cecilia asked dully.

"I think you know precisely what I'm talking about, Cecilia," he replied.

Cecilia looked up at Evan's towering frame. His face was set in arctic severity, his only discernible emotion a kind of impassive hatred. Cecilia had never seen him like this, and she felt stunned.

"I owe an apology to the family for my own behavior," Evan resumed, "but, given my discoveries, I will take solace in knowing that I've acted in time to forestall true disaster."

A glimmer of understanding pushed through Cecilia's bewilderment. She sensed that Evan was accusing her of something. "What are you talking about?" she repeated.

Evan's eyes locked with hers for a split second before he answered, but even the loathing in his gaze couldn't prepare her for what followed. "I'm talking about your attempts to destroy Chesterton Manor," he accused.

Cecilia was speechless. She glanced questioningly around the room. No one spoke. The faces revealed nothing. Did the others know what he had planned to say? What was happening couldn't be real, she told herself numbly.

Evan's voice reached through the vacuum of silence. "I owe the family an apology because it was my responsibility and no one else's to check Cecilia's references. Beyond this, I have shown myself to be a poor judge of character. I should have thought more carefully about Cecilia's background before engaging her as a tour guide. I alone bear the burden of having brought this wild girl into our home. Fortunately the police have helped to bring me to my senses."

Still no one else spoke, and Evan continued. "I know now, Cecilia, that it was you who arranged for the disaster at the bridge this afternoon. And I believe that I have discovered your accomplice in the crime. The police, as I said, have been very helpful."

"You're mad!" Cecilia breathed.

"You must be," Emily said, coming to Cecilia's defense. "What in heaven's name are you talking about?"

Evan's words seemed to echo off the ornate walls and the high ceiling as he made his case. "Miss Bennett, as we all know recently arrived in England from Kenya. She was raised far from the context of English social graces—and learned quite naturally, to thrive on the excitement and brutality of the wild. Could you, for example, Cecilia, hunt, kill and serve an animal for our dinner if we were hungry enough?"

"Of course...I have skills that are suited to a life away from the comforts of the city and all the modern conveniences," Cecilia said in wide-eyed reply. "But what does that have to do with the bridge?"

"Nothing," Evan conceded with a self-satisfied smile. "I just didn't want to give you an opportunity to lie by knowing the purpose of my question—as you did lie about your age when you knew I would hire only an applicant who was twenty-one years of age." Evan paused to light a cigarette, then continued with some relish: "I know that it was you who slaughtered the cows, as well. I just wanted you to establish before the others that you're capable of such an act."

"You've established nothing!" Emily cried in amazement. "You yourself, Evan, would know how to kill two defenseless cows. But that doesn't mean that you're capable of such an act!"

"Let him finish," Catherine interjected eagerly. Then, seemingly conscious of her tone, she added, "I'm sure we'd all like to see Cecilia's character cleared."

Tony suddenly ran across the room and threw himself into Cecilia's armchair. Absently she made room for him, knowing that the boy wanted to give her his support. Her eyes, however, were fixed on Evan's pacing form. How could she ever have loved him?

"Evan?" Philip ventured softly, "aren't you getting a bit extravagant here?"

"No, Philip, I'm not. And if the family would just keep silent for a few moments I'll be able to make this all clear."

Cecilia felt her thick eyelashes moisten. She dared not blink. The tears would flow. What was Evan doing to her? Surely he must at least suspect the truth—suspect that Catherine was behind all the attacks on Chesterton. The situation had been going on for more than a year. How could Evan believe that she, Cecilia, had anything to do with it?

"You see," Evan continued, "Cecilia Bennett didn't need to take the job of tour guide at Chesterton Manor. In fact, she has several thousand dollars in cash hidden right here in her suite. How much more she has hidden away in some bank in London I don't know. But Cecilia could live quite well without the salary or the tips she receives here.

"No, Cecilia wanted something besides a livelihood out of Chesterton. She wanted excitement. And she's created plenty of just that. She most certainly was the one who slaughtered the cows. And as I have said, I happen to know that she has an accomplice. She has skillfully worked her way into the brutal underworld of Devonshire county. Recently she met with one of the most unsavory of Dartmouth's criminals, though I haven't tried to speculate on what binds her to this man—except a love of destruction. I believe you loaned Cecilia your car a few nights ago,

Emily. It was on that very night that the two conspired.

"Fortunately the reputation of this man is well known to the police, and they were kind enough to tell me that in their routine surveillance of him they'd observed his meeting with Cecilia. They suspected a plot against the members of the Cedric-Browne family.

"That was when I began to research Cecilia's past. Shortly after, I discovered the money she had hidden—or at least the cash portion of it. The money told me that Cecilia had ulterior motives for acting as tour guide here, but it was only when the bridge collapsed that I knew what Cecilia and this man had been planning. The police verified this afternoon that several of the beams in the bridge had been sawed. They estimated that the work had been done a few days ago and that it was only a matter of time before the bridge would collapse.

"Finally, that man was here today. Like Cecilia, he was conveniently located at the edge of the bridge when it collapsed. He pulled a few people to safety before they could slide into the water and these people provided an excellent description of him. For you see, he didn't wait to be questioned by the police. He fled the scene of the crime."

"Cecilia was hurt, Evan!" Emily cried in disbelief. "You *can't* believe that she's behind this. Look at her bandaged ankle!"

"I know Cecilia was hurt. But she'll live. Won't you, Cecilia?" Evan asked wryly. "And it was exciting, wasn't it? Dangerous?" he persisted.

"So you're saying that Cecilia came to Chesterton with a sizable quantity of cash," Catherine said pensively, "just so that she could satisfy a lust for danger, under the guise of tour guide? And I suppose that destruction and sabotage are easier to bring off in the countryside than in a city with the sophistication of London..." she mused.

"You're catching on," Evan said with obvious satisfaction.

Cecilia felt the first tears fall. The injustice of Evan's attack was staggering. She had never before in her life felt so betrayed, so wronged. Evan was twisting everything she had told him in confidence on that sultry night in his study. How had she managed to misjudge him so completely? She had thought that he was wise and kind. She had credited him with great burdens, burdens that were somehow bound up in his love of others—including Emily and Tony.

And how had he found out about her hidden money—and her dinner with Hillary, if indeed he was alluding to that night? Did he really believe that Hillary was a criminal? Surely the police had said nothing of the kind. But Hillary had run from the scene of the accident. He'd had to. Emily could not see him. Not under the circumstances.

With a start Cecilia realized that the entire family was staring at her. The tears fell silently down her cheeks. She refused to defend herself. It would be hopeless. Nothing would make her betray Hillary as Evan had betrayed her. She would have to find Hillary and tell him what had happened. Then it would be up to him to carry on. She herself would have to leave Chesterton in the morning. Evan had spoken, and she had witnessed before the power he wielded over the family. No one would seriously challenge him.

Cecilia struggled to lift herself from the armchair. Tony pulled at her arm, but she felt nothing when she put all her weight on her injured ankle. She lifted the brown envelope containing the tour money and walked to the center of the room, where she faced Evan. Her thick lashes were drenched with tears. She couldn't see his eyes, nor did she want to.

In one graceful motion she emptied the envelope at his feet. The bills drifted to the floor. The coins echoed in the immense empty room.

"That is the last of the tour money that you shall receive from my hand or my enterprise," she said hoarsely. "I will leave first thing in the morning—providing, to be sure, a forwarding address so that you and the good constables of Dartmouth can pursue me if you ever manage to build a case against me."

Behind her Cecilia could hear Tony let out a little cry. She heard his feet pounding on the floor as he ran to Emily.

"As for my 'fortune,' it shall remain hidden to the last. I rightly suspected that there was a thief at Chesterton, and the money will be added to my suitcase only in the final minutes before I leave. I will leave with a clear conscience—and a deep sense of hatred and betrayal."

Control was no longer possible. Cecilia ran from the salon, oblivious to the shouts of Emily and Tony and to the pain in her ankle.

For nearly a minute Cecilia was completely disoriented. Why was there someone knocking at her door? It was night. What was she doing in the chair in her sitting room, she wondered, and why were her eyes so sore?

Emily burst into the room, and it all came back. She had cried for an eternity when she had returned to her room; she must have fallen asleep in the chair. Evan had betrayed her. The man she loved was everything she had feared initially, and more.

"Cecilia," Emily begged, "wake up." The woman switched on the light, and Cecilia blinked furiously. "Evan's hurt. You must come!" She continued urgently.

"Evan?" was all Cecilia could manage.

"Yes, yes, his associate—the man with the black beard—called me. He had a message from Evan. They were on a job and Evan was shot. Nick just called with a message from Evan."

"On a job?" Cecilia struggled to sit up in the chair. Was she being asked to assist Evan in escaping a criminal act after what he had done to her?

"Yes," Emily continued breathlessly. "Evan said to tell you that he's sorry. Please come—he needs you," she begged. "They couldn't go to the police. Not yet. Nick left Evan in the orchard."

Evan was sorry...and he needed her. Just a few hours earlier the words would have been music to Cecilia's ears.

"Please, Cecilia," Emily persisted. "He asked for *you*."

"Let's go," was all Cecilia said.

Chapter 11

"Where are you going?" Emily demanded as Cecilia turned toward the formal garden.

"To the stable."

"Evan's in the orchard!"

"And how do you think we're going to get a wounded man of Evan's size to safety?"

"I don't know," Emily said slowly, but she didn't move.

"On Tchaikovsky. He's the only horse in the stable that—"

"I won't have it!" Emily interrupted. Then, more kindly, she said, "Cecilia, it's impossible."

Cecilia sighed heavily, the sound made loud by the stillness of the night. "I didn't plan to tell you like this," she began. "In fact, after what happened tonight I don't know how I would have ever got the news to you. But here goes—I've trained Tchaikovsky. He's as gentle as a lamb. A big lamb." Cecilia's happy moment was anticlimactic. She had waited so long for the right moment to tell Emily. Now her achievement felt empty.

When Emily did not reply Cecilia added, "You can go wake up Tony if you need verification. I've ridden Tchaikovsky every morning at dawn since that crisis in the stable. One morning Tony even rode with me."

Suddenly Emily's arms flew around Cecilia. "I believe you, Cecilia. I'm just speechless. You're wonderful. And I've known it—somehow I've known it since that first morning when I was so rude to you. Thank you for Tchaikovsky. Thank you!"

Even through the deep sorrow that Cecilia felt at how things had ended for her at Chesterton, Emily's thanks felt good. She gave the woman a reassuring hug. She was leaving as she had wished—Emily and Tony, at least, had been given hope.

"I want you to understand," Emily began through the soft tears that were falling down her face, "I have to tell you—"

"Later," Cecilia interrupted gently. "We have to get to Evan now."

Emily nodded, and the pair broke into a loping run through the formal garden. Cecilia grimaced at the pain in her ankle. She prayed that the stitches would not give way, but she was grateful for the exercise. Her head was clearing.

When they'd reached the stable Cecilia went straight to Tchaikovsky's stall. Emily produced a flashlight from somewhere in the mess of equipment on a worktable.

"I sometimes come down here and look at him in the night," she whispered. "The flashlight...." Her words trailed off as, spellbound, she watched Cecilia gently

pat the great mahogany neck of the horse, willing him
to wake up calmly in a moment when calm was essen-
tial. She had no idea how badly Evan was injured or
why she was running to his rescue.

"Come on out," Cecilia said softly to the massive
horse as she led him from the stall. "Your mistress
and I need you. You don't mind an extra rider, do
you?"

Cecilia motioned for Emily to approach the horse.
Emily hesitated. But Cecilia's mastery of the scene was
complete. Within moments they were riding through
the night, Cecilia at the reins and Emily holding on for
dear life.

Once in the orchard, Emily automatically switched
on the flashlight. It didn't take them long to find Evan.
He was slumped against one of the trees, but his eyes
fluttered open at the sound of their approach. In the
strange light of the flashlight Cecilia saw alarm cross
his face when he realized that they'd traveled on
Tchaikovsky's back. Cecilia jumped down off the
horse and tossed the reins to Emily.

"Why did you bring...how will you ever..." Evan
stammered in confusion.

Cecilia knelt by his side. "You didn't want us to
wake up the whole household, did you?" she asked
briskly. "Emily and I could never have carried you
back to the house—and neither could any of the other
horses in that shabby stable Mathias keeps. Even your
tiny excuse for a car," she added with a glimmer of a
smile, "couldn't slip between these trees."

"But Tchaikovsky?" Evan said in wonder.

"Cecilia trained him—at sunrise every morning.

Tony knew all about it," Emily said excitedly. "Oh, Evan, you were right to trust Cecilia tonight!"

"And very wrong to betray me this evening," Cecilia added dryly as she began to inspect the wound in Evan's shoulder. "Bring me the flashlight closer," she instructed Emily.

"Cecilia, I have to—" Evan began.

"I'd love to hear your explanation later," Cecilia said, "but you're not going to be able to give it if you lose any more blood."

She dared not look into Evan's eyes. She wanted to get him to safety, to hear what he was about to say, but she couldn't allow herself to be distracted. And she had to move fast.

"I can't do anything for him here," she called over her shoulder to Emily. "We'll have to get him up on Tchaikovsky and take him back to my suite."

Following Cecilia's orders, Emily helped to get Evan up on the horse. She bent down on all fours, making a table of her body, while Cecilia guided Evan up onto the horse. It required tremendous strength of both Emily and Cecilia. Evan was not deadweight, but he was too weak to offer much help. Cecilia had to provide all the support she could to keep Emily from bending under the weight of her brother as he mounted the horse.

There was only room for one more rider on the horse, and Cecilia was the obvious choice as Tchaikovsky's trainer. Careful not to disturb Evan any more than necessary, she climbed on behind him. The ride would be made all the more difficult, she knew, because it was not safe to depend on Evan to ride in the back and hold onto her. She would have to guide Tchaikovsky from behind Evan's limp body while trying to hold Evan steady. Emily suggested that it would be too risky to take Evan directly to the manor. Someone might hear Tchaikovsky. The garden approach, she insisted, was safer. Cecilia agreed and Emily handed the flashlight up to her, saying that she knew a shortcut back to the stable. She promised to beat them there.

And she did. Cecilia took the ride very slowly. Once Evan tried to speak, but she silenced him. She could not risk his losing any more strength while she had the responsibility to hold him in the saddle. So great was the concentration required to get them safely back to the stable that she had only one thought on the laborious trip: Tchaikovsky was behaving perfectly. Cecilia was warmed by intense pride in what she had achieved with the animal. Then her thoughts focused on the next task at hand.

"You made it!" Emily cried softly as they reached the doors of the stable.

"Yes," Evan said his voice almost inaudible. "We made it."

"Clear a space on that worktable," Cecilia ordered, "so that we can bring him down in stages."

Emily complied and soon Evan stood shakily, supported by the table, his sister and Cecilia.

Cecilia wavered for only a moment. Then she handed the reins to Emily. "Take Tchaikovsky back into his stall while I hold Evan," she instructed.

A look of fear spread across Emily's face, but she took the reins and gave them a gentle tug. Tchaikovsky responded at once. In less than a minute the trio was struggling through the garden.

When they arrived at Cecilia's suite they heaved a collective sigh of relief. Emily opened the door, and the instant the two women had lowered Evan into the armchair Cecilia swayed and sank into the facing chair. She caught her breath and inspected her ankle. The pain was acute, but the stitches had held.

"Do you have some alcohol and bandages?" she asked Emily, pulling herself together.

Emily nodded and dashed from the room.

Cecilia leaned over Evan, and his eyes opened to meet hers. Even through clouds of pain Cecilia could read his thanks. She knew she was looking into the eyes of the man she loved—a man who needed her and who had also been unspeakably cruel to her.

She surveyed the wound. There was a great deal of blood, most of it dried. The bleeding was only slight now, but Evan's black shirt was dampened over a wide area. She ripped open the shirt to expose the wound, then hurried to the bathroom. After drenching her bath towel in warm water she ran back into the sitting room. Gently she began to wash away the dried blood until she could see the injured area clearly.

From time to time she glanced from the wound to Evan's face. He was watching her every movement. Relieved to be out of the orchard and in the safety of the manor, he was recovering his strength rapidly.

"Here's the alcohol," Emily said breathlessly, "and all the bandages I could find." Then she added, "We're not very well supplied with this kind of thing."

Cecilia grunted slightly in acknowledgment. "I've worked with less," she said.

"Are you a nurse?" Emily asked, curious.

"No, just good at first aid," Cecilia replied as she opened the bottle of alcohol. Then she couldn't resist saying, "When you have a lust for danger and destruction as I do, you have to be talented at putting back together all the people you shoot in moments of frenzied abandon."

Evan spoke for the first time since they'd reached the manor. "Cecilia, you have to understand—"

"Not now. Not yet," Cecilia interrupted. "First things first. This is going to hurt."

Evan stiffened in the chair as Cecilia drenched the area of the wound with alcohol. Painstakingly she moved the cotton back and forth, gently erasing as best she could the possibility of infection.

Evan did not make a sound, but the beads of sweat that formed on his forehead bore testimony to the extreme control he was exercising. Out of the corner of her eye Cecilia saw Emily turn away, unable to watch the process of cleansing the ugly gash.

"You were lucky," Cecilia said as she put aside the last wad of cotton. "The bullet entered in a straight course just under your shoulder bone and passed out your back without even touching your shoulder blade. Your left arm will be useless to you for a while, and you'll still need to see a doctor—but I'm glad for both our sakes that I didn't have to remove the bullet tonight."

She turned to Emily. "We'll have to get him to sit up a little more in the chair so that I can put on a proper bandage."

Before Emily could get to the chair Evan was pulling himself up into position. Cecilia stopped him at once. "Don't try to make things worse!" she scolded. "I said you were lucky. I didn't say that the wound wasn't deep, the bullet went through your shoulder, for God's sake! Any exertion and—"

"I'm much better," Evan breathed.

Emily and Cecilia lifted Evan up a few more inches, then Cecilia began to wind the white bandage under Evan's arm covering the wound entirely.

"Why are you doing this?" Evan said faintly.

"You called for me, didn't you?" Cecilia said.

"But I had no right to—"

"No, you didn't," Cecilia snapped. "Yourself a criminal—and you draw upon confidences to try to frame me for—"

"Evan's not a criminal!" Emily protested.

"Oh, no?" Cecilia said dryly. "Ask him about the night he picked me up at the station. Ask him about what he and his 'associate,' Nick, were doing the night Benningsway was robbed. Ask him—"

"I now what they were doing!" Emily interrupted. "Evan and Nick are working as security consultants to the wealthy estates in the area. They have been ever since this crime wave started."

It was Cecilia's turn to be shocked. She held the roll of bandages in midair.

"I knew it was too risky, Evan. You should have left it to the police. All the money you've earned is not worth *this!*" Emily thrust a hand in the direction of Evan's shoulder. Cecilia still held the bandage in her hand, motionless.

"Chesterton would never have survived these past few months if I hadn't done something myself," Evan said wanly.

"Why couldn't you tell me?" Cecilia said in dismay. "I believed that you were—"

"An art thief," Evan finished. "I suspected as much." He paused and swayed as if struck by a wave of pain, then continued, "Why didn't you confront me?"

Cecilia shook her head. It was all too much. Absently she began to twist the bandage around Evan's shoulder again. "I was going to," she said at last. "That night in the study when you . . . when you . . ."

"When I kissed you," Evan sighed.

"You love her, don't you, Evan?" Emily asked softly. "I know you do. That's why I don't understand what came over you this evening when you—"

"Please, Emily," Evan said. "Give me time. I didn't plan to be away this evening—or to have everything imaginable go wrong at Hathaway."

Cecilia tore off a piece of adhesive tape and applied it to the bandage where the gauze ended, taking care to put pressure on the tape in a place that was least likely to be tender.

"Is Nick all right?" Emily asked suddenly. "When he called he sounded—"

"Busy, I'm sure," Evan supplied. "Yes, he's all right. Or at least he was. Everything got out of hand. We had almost no notice that the hit was going to take place. Our sources have been better in the past. Anyway, we got into a shooting match and it was all Nick could do to drop me in the orchard. If he'd tried to get me to a hospital in Dartmouth he would have had to stray too far from their trail, and the hospital would have reported a gunshot victim immediately to the police, who would have ruined. . . ." Evan's voice trailed off, his strength sapped by the agitation of remembering the scene.

Emily was curled up on the floor by Evan's side, and she placed a protective hand on her brother's knee, then turned to Cecilia. "Evan and Nick were classmates at Cambridge," she explained. "Nick's field of study was criminology, but I guess he took an early interest in art, too. He was one of your students, right, Evan?" she asked. Evan nodded and Emily continued, "Anyway, Nick asked Evan to be a partner in his firm so that he could take on the protection of art treasures, because Evan knows all about art. That's pretty much the story, isn't it, Evan?"

"Yes, it is," Evan conceded. "Could I please have a cigarette?"

Cecilia sighed, but lighted one and handed it to Evan. She could see that Evan was feeling much better.

"Emily," Evan began, "can I trouble you to bring me something from the kitchen? I'm not really hungry, but I'd like something hot. A cup of coffee with a good shot of brandy would be perfect."

Emily was on her feet at once. "Be right back," she promised, already on her way out of the suite.

"Not too soon, dear sister," Evan whispered to himself. Then he lifted his eyes to Cecilia. "I have to talk with Cecilia," he explained.

Cecilia said nothing. She was amazed by Evan's strange behavior. Yet she could see him risking his life for the manor, taking on a job that involved great danger so that he could earn the great sums attendant with that danger. And she now saw why he had been so secretive. He had obviously built up the myth of his gambling successes to deceive everyone in the household save Emily. There was no one else he could trust, and he had no way of knowing whether or not Cecilia would befriend Catherine, so he had kept her in the dark, too. Perhaps he would have told her that night in the study . . . if she had not run from his arms.

"I've made a terrible mess of things," Evan said wearily, "but I haven't much time to explain. I sent Emily to the kitchen because I knew she wouldn't stop at coffee. She'll be a while preparing an unnecessary feast for me—and I need every minute of that time to make you understand."

"Understand what?" Cecilia said warily. Could he possibly have an explanation for the way he had behaved earlier, in the salon?

"Hillary called me after the bridge collapsed," he said. His eyes sought an ashtray, and mechanically Cecilia extended one to him. "He was frantic about the disaster—because it proved that Catherine would stop at nothing, that she would endanger lives, including yours."

"Did he tell you . . . ." Cecilia began in wonder.

"He told me everything. And I feel like a perfect fool for not tracking him down months ago for Emily's sake. But that's behind us. We have a great deal to do in the present."

"We?" Cecilia questioned. "But I thought you thought I killed the cows and rigged the bridge—"

"Oh, I thought nothing of the kind!" Evan exclaimed, and he moved sharply in the chair, wincing in pain as he did so. "And it gave me no pleasure to pretend that I did. But think, Cecilia. It will be several days before the bridge is fixed and the tours can begin again. In that time Catherine is certain to increase her demands for the sale of Chesterton. She'll feel she's almost won—and the tour-money scheme was the best and safest way to trip her up. Without the tours she might try one last stunt, much more harmful than all the rest. We couldn't risk that. We had to have a more confined scheme."

"We?" Cecilia said again. "I don't understand."

"Mathias and Catherine will stop at nothing. I see that now. I should have caught on sooner, but it's been difficult enough just trying to keep Chesterton going and handling the work I've been doing with Nick, not to mention pretending that I'm a gambler and a writer and—" Evan broke off. The strain of trying to say so much so quickly was taking its toll.

Cecilia leaned over to put a restraining hand on his arm. "Be quiet for a moment," she said softly. "So Hillary called you and told you of his conclusions and his fears. He told you about the plan he and I had formed to catch Catherine stealing the tour money. Then, after the bridge collapse, you and Hillary changed the plan. That scene in the salon about how I was a savage from Africa was part of your new plan. Nod if I'm right so far."

Evan nodded.

"You don't want to be the one to tell Emily that Hillary is involved with Chesterton again. You want Hillary to do that himself, so you sent her to the kitchen to give you time to fill me in. If you hadn't been called away to Hathaway this evening you would have been able to tell me right after you discredited me before your family?"

"Yes," Evan murmured. "All that nonsense about your money was bait for Catherine. I didn't want to tell you before I staged that horrible scene, because I was afraid it wouldn't look convincing if you knew. But I was going to set things up for tomorrow as soon as...."

"As soon as you could," Cecilia finished. She moved to Evan's side. "I'm to stage things tomorrow so that Catherine knows that I've packed—and put the money in my suitcase. Hillary will get Philip, and they'll hide in the bedroom of this suite, just as we'd planned about the tour money. Am I right?"

Again Evan nodded.

"If everything goes according to plan Catherine will slip into the sitting room as soon as she gets a chance, fearing my return. And when she takes the money, Hillary and Philip will be witnesses to the theft. Philip has to be made to see once and for all that his pretty young wife is the cause of all the bad that's happened."

"I should have trusted you sooner," Evan said. "I should never have let you run from the study that night."

For a moment neither of them spoke. Then, almost against her will, Cecilia asked, "Who's the woman who's so dear to you? Why aren't you in a position to love me?" She wanted to call back her words the instant she spoke them, but it was too late.

Evan looked confused, and his bushy eyebrows drew together in puzzlement.

"You fixed the windshield to hide the truth from someone you loved that first night," Cecilia went on. She didn't want to hear the truth, but she knew she had to. "And in the study you said—".

"The woman I love is you, Cecilia, only you. I was protecting Emily—I didn't want to worry her with the knowledge that we had been shot at." Evan raised his hand, tenderly brushing back a wisp of dark hair that had fallen over Cecilia's face. "That night in the study...I didn't want to involve you. But couldn't you see...couldn't you see, every day, how much I love you?"

Cecilia felt the tears forming in her eyes. A tear dropped on Evan's hand, then the hand slipped down to her chin and he drew her mouth to his. Their lips touched, and she felt the warm urgency of his kiss. She wanted desperately to fall into his arms....

Cecilia jumped at the sound of the door opening. It was Emily. Evan's sister smiled when she saw them. She walked over to the small round table beside Evan's chair, where she put down a large tray. She'd brought a bowl of steaming soup, hot rolls and butter, cheese and cold meats—and a pot of coffee, next to which sat a bottle of Courvoisier.

"I thought you might need a little more than coffee," she said shyly, "to get your strength back."

Chapter 12

Everything was in place, Cecilia thought to herself; if only her heart would stop beating so wildly. Ten-thirty, Evan had said. Emily had given Evan and Cecilia a few minutes alone last night after he'd had some soup and drunk coffee mixed with brandy. But they had had no time to talk of love. Hurriedly Evan had sketched out the details of what he and Hillary had planned earlier that day.

Cecilia was to find out from Gwen where Catherine was likely to be at ten-thirty. It was Hillary's task to persuade Philip—who was certain to be found in the garden—to accompany him to Cecilia's suite and hide in the bedroom. Philip would be told only that the thief was expected and that a trap had been laid.

Cecilia hoped that Hillary would be able to succeed. Evan was sound asleep in his bedroom, recovering from the strain of the previous night, so he could not be counted on to get his brother into the suite as originally planned. For her part, Cecilia had had no trouble learning Catherine's plans from Gwen.

Now all she had to do was "accidentally" bump into Catherine and tell her that she was packed and ready to leave shortly. Then she would explain that she wanted to say goodbye to Tony. Cecilia could only hope that Tony would be playing in his favorite spot in the woods, not far from the manor. It would spoil everything if the boy were near Catherine. But that was unlikely. And it was also something they could do nothing about.

Cecilia glanced at her watch. Ten twenty-nine. She adjusted the collar of her blue linen traveling suit and headed for the door. Hillary would be approaching Philip now.

The back door stuck slightly when Cecilia tried to open it. The wood had swollen in the summer's humidity. She gave it a little kick, then grimaced and looked down at her ankle. A bit of blood had seeped through the bandage. She pushed the door again and stepped out into the bright sunlight.

Catherine was exactly where Gwen had said she would be—on the lower terrace of the west wing, doing her nails. Cecilia found it amazing that Gwen had known precisely where Catherine would be and exactly what she would be doing. That Catherine would follow a routine so rigidly that she could be found on the same day of each week doing her nails on the terrace seemed remarkable. But Gwen was unmistakably right.

Cecilia closed the door heavily. As intended, the noise attracted Catherine's attention.

"Over here," she called, waving her arm above

her head, "Cecilia, come let me wish you goodbye."

Cecilia smiled to herself and strolled over to where Catherine was stretched out on a chaise longue. She wore a crocheted bikini and a covering gown of red silky material. The gown was fastened only at her waist, and the full-length skirt fell open, exposing her well-tanned legs.

"You must forgive me," Catherine fussed. "I know I look a fright, what with my hair stuck every which way on top of my head, but I had no idea you were leaving so soon."

"In a matter of minutes," Cecilia informed her. "I've packed all my things. Emily's taking me to the station. I just wanted to see if Tony was in his usual spot in the woods," she said, looking down dejectedly, "so that I could say goodbye to him personally before we left."

"Oh, of course. I'm sure it will mean a great deal to him," Catherine said in a low voice. She squinted up into the sun at Cecilia and added, "Though I think he might have gone a little farther out today. The bridge episode yesterday upset him quite a lot, as I'm sure it did you."

"Yes," Cecilia agreed. "I know he's upset." For a second Cecilia thought she was about to remember where she thought she'd seen Catherine before. Something about the way her face was contorted as she looked up into the sun, perhaps. Then the moment passed. She couldn't catch the memory. "I've got to be on my way," she said finally. "Emily will have my forwarding address in London."

"And I'll be sure to call on you," Catherine said, swinging her glistening legs around to touch the slate slabs of the terrace. "I ought to be checking with Gwen on the luncheon menu," she went on, "but do have a smooth ride back into the city." She started to extend her hand, then drew it back, waving the bottle of nail polish before Cecilia and indicating her blood-red nails.

Cecilia smiled. "I understand. Have a nice summer, Catherine."

The words were hardly out of her mouth before Catherine had placed her sticky nails around the doorknob that would open her way back into the manor.

Cecilia watched her go inside, then slowly walked back across the gravel parking lot, her feet crunching on the tiny stones. She didn't have much time. And Catherine was obviously not wasting any time. No one would jump up right in the middle of doing her nails to consult a maid about a menu that wouldn't be relevant for more than two hours—least of all Catherine, Cecilia thought nervously.

At the corner of the east wing Cecilia paused. She didn't need to find Tony now. There would be plenty of time to see him later. Right now she needed to be perfectly certain of her timing. Everything was going according to plan, and her nerves calmed. Catherine could not have been more on cue if she had been supplied with a script.

Timing. Slowly Cecilia edged her way along the back wall of the manor. The coarse red brick caught her skirt once, and she pulled the linen free. Cautiously she peered through the window, the one in which she had first seen Nick's bearded face. Then she had been concerned that Evan and the frightening man were somehow engaged in crime together. But now she tried to look through the window in such a way as to make it impossible for anyone to see her from the inside. Cecilia could feel the nervousness returning as her muscles tensed to hold the unnatural position.

She didn't have to wait long. A blur of red swished into view. At the end of the hall Catherine was already entering her suite.

Cecilia counted to ten. *Let Catherine open the suitcase,* she prayed. *Let Hillary stop Philip from bursting into the open the minute he sees Catherine.* Cecilia clearly wanted to see Catherine put her hands on the thick stacks of cash.

Ten. Cecilia twisted the knob of the door. It stuck again, and she drew a deep breath. This time she leaned heavily against the wood with her hip, at the same time bracing the door so it wouldn't fly open suddenly, giving away her entry. The door gave. Noiselessly she tiptoed down the short hallway. She opened the door to her suite.

"Cecilia!" Catherine cried. She let a stack of bills fall from her hand to the open suitcase. Her face was no longer beautiful. It was pulled into an angry accusation, an accusation combining hatred, fear and guilt. "I thought you were going to say goodbye to Tony!"

Hillary and Philip stepped out of the bedroom. Cecilia's eyes met Hillary's and she sagged against the wall by the door. The look of confidence on Hillary's face assured her that Philip had seen everything.

Catherine followed Cecilia's gaze, and she staggered slightly at the sight of her husband. "Philip! And Hillary Masterson—the thief!"

Hillary laughed softly. "The thief," he repeated wonderingly.

"Why, you've all framed me!" Catherine shouted. "You've made it look as if . . . as if . . . ."

"As if you were the thief?" Hillary supplied.

Cecilia's eyes shifted to Philip. Deep sorrow filled his face, a sorrow mixed with self-hatred. "Catherine, how could you?" he said at last.

Catherine turned on her heel and started for the door. Philip let out a loud wail. In two steps he had reached Catherine. He grabbed her wrist and twirled her around to face him. "How could you?" he demanded. "How could you!" The words were garbled by the tremendous grief he was experiencing, but still, they were plain for all to hear.

Catherine wilted slightly under the tightness of her husband's grip. At once he dropped her hand. His head hung.

"Philip, darling," Catherine begged, "don't you see what's happening?" She crept up to her husband and put her slender hands on his soft rounded shoulders. "Darling, these two troublemakers are just trying to spoil our love. I was only checking to make sure that no one had disturbed Cecilia's things—otherwise she might have claimed that her money had been stolen and expected Chesterton to replace the sum." Catherine stretched up on her toes and rubbed her cheek against Philip's. "I was just trying to protect us, Philip, dear."

Philip took a step back, and Catherine's hands fell away. "It's no use, Catherine," he said angrily. "I see now what a fool I've been. You've wanted me to sell

Chesterton all along—ever since the day we met. Oh, how you convinced me," he moaned. "I so wanted you to really love me. But you never had any intention of loving me or Chesterton or Tony. Every time something was looking up you contrived to ruin it. Hillary was going to rebuild the name of the Chesterton stables—and you framed him. Cecilia had made a thriving enterprise out of the tours—and you robbed her."

"It's not true, darling," Catherine protested. "You can't believe what you're saying."

Cecilia was impressed by the smoothness of Catherine's performance. She thought fleetingly that if anyone could dissuade Philip from the truth, Catherine could.

"I don't understand it at all," Philip went on sadly. "Evan has been telling me that something was wrong, but I didn't believe him. I didn't want to...."

Cecilia was filled with pity for Philip. His devastation was complete, and she knew that he'd been incapable of dealing with the situation from the beginning.

"Hillary," Philip said, turning slightly. "Please go to Emily. I know it will mean the world to her to learn that I've relented, to hear you explain how wrongly I—"

Hillary put his hand on Philip's shoulder. "Don't say any more, Philip. I understand." He strode across the room to the door, and when he reached Cecilia he leaned down and kissed her cheek. "Thank you, Cecilia," he whispered. For the first time Cecilia saw a ray of happiness penetrate his deep gray eyes. Then she heard him hurry down the great hallway in search of Emily.

"Cecilia," Philip continued, raising his head to gaze across the room, "I don't understand what Evan was getting at last night in the salon, but I don't feel I have the strength to face that problem at the moment. I do hope you'll stay, though, for a few hours, at least." Philip lowered his eyes again. His voice was a whisper when next he spoke. "I need time to think. To be alone." With that he crossed to the door.

"Philip, darling!" Catherine screamed. "Oh, my poor, poor Philip!"

To Cecilia, Catherine's anguish sounded shockingly genuine. How they had underestimated Catherine!

Philip pushed wordlessly past Cecilia, and Catherine rushed after him. Cecilia watched the defeated man plod his way down the hall while Catherine, her red gown flowing, fluttered after him, moaning and pleading like a scorned butterfly. Cecilia closed her door on the scene.

Looking around the room where so much had happened, she suddenly experienced an intense wave of loneliness. She was happy to think of the joy that Hillary and Emily must be sharing at this very minute. And she knew that Chesterton was safe at last. No one would take the manor from Tony.

But she needed Evan. Her moment of triumph felt empty without him. She had risked so much for her love—her love of Evan and Tony and Emily and Chesterton. The manor had felt like home to her, an unsafe home but still a home that she had vowed to fight for.

She glanced at the piles of clothes scattered around

her suitcase. Catherine had wasted no time in digging for the money. Cecilia felt a deadening fatigue sweep over her, and she knew the fatigue to be borne of disappointment. The silly disappointment that Evan, who was still recovering, was not with her now. She didn't know what the future would hold for them, but after last night she felt fairly certain that things would work out well. If Evan loved her nothing could stand in their way, especially with Catherine exposed.

Suddenly she had an idea. Of all the rooms in the manor, it was the gallery that she most associated with Evan. She remembered the admiration she had felt for him on that first day, when he had talked of the portraiture art. The thought of the way he had made fun of her when she had been transfixed by the dazzling portrait of Lady Eleanora made her smile. Somehow Cecilia sensed Evan's spirit would be in the gallery. If she couldn't be with him physically, she wanted to be in his favorite room.

Without a second thought Cecilia left the sitting room and mounted the stairs to the second floor. When she reached the gallery she knew she'd been right. Evan's presence seemed to fill the room. The bright vibrant colors of the oil paintings strongly reminded her of Evan. Cecilia drifted over to the portraits of Reginald and Eleanora. The late-morning light made the room glow, picking up the touch of each brushstroke, the power of the bold tones of the paintings. Evan had been right. No one had ever asked her who had painted these two particular portraits. She smiled, thinking to herself that Rollings de Stangrave was doomed to anonymity. Evan was far too modest. . . .

She took a few steps back from the immense canvases and rested gently against one of the low glass display cases. Lady Eleanora had indeed been a beautiful woman, she thought idly. Beautiful and deadly.

A shrill laugh cut through Cecilia's musing. She turned automatically in the direction of the sound. Catherine stood blocking the only entrance to the gallery.

"How charming!" Catherine exclaimed. "I was just looking for you so that I could persuade you to take a little walk to the gallery with me—and here you are, right where I want you." Again Catherine laughed. It was a menacing sound, and Cecilia made to leave.

"Not so close," Catherine cautioned. Out of the folds of her red gown a heavy blue black revolver emerged. Cecilia froze at the sight of the weapon. Then she took several steps backward.

"That's better," Catherine said softly, "much better." She drew closer to Cecilia, then continued. "You've been an enormous amount of trouble, Miss Cecilia Bennett. An enormous amount." Her blue eyes shone hard and cold in the sunlight, and the golden curls piled on top of her head gave her a wild look. "It made me sick," she hissed, "to see the crowds pouring into this place for your stupid tours. You had to be so clever, too, with those foreign-language tours. And you had to be stopped.

"But you weren't as easy as the others," Catherine went on. "Seeing the tour money disappear one or two times was enough for all of them. Oh, a few tried to replace the money with their own, but all of them gave in eventually. Lots of thieves left Chesterton in disgrace last summer, and that troublemaker Evan was so busy gambling his nights away that he didn't have a chance to see what was happening."

Cecilia eyed the revolver warily. A fresh wave of fear swept over her as she judged the distance between herself and Catherine. It was hopeless. Catherine was too far away. And Catherine had the position of strength. All she would have to do would be strike Cecilia with the revolver's heavy grip.

"But Evan played right into my hands this time," Catherine said triumphantly. "How nice to have him on my side for once. He's a powerful ally, you know. And a powerful enemy. Last night's exposure of your 'lust for danger' was pure ecstasy for me, Cecilia. But Evan didn't go far enough. I can see that there's only one way to deal with you." Catherine paused, and Cecilia held her breath. The woman was mad!

"Finally," Catherine said, "so that I can forget all about you."

"You'll never get away with it, Catherine," Cecilia pleaded.

"Of course I will," Catherine replied easily. "But Mathias will take care of you. He did such a nice job with the cows and the bridge and...oh, lots of things you don't even know about. A talented man, my Mathias."

"You didn't hear me, Catherine," Cecilia asserted. "I said you'll never get away with this. Evan knows the truth. So do Hillary and Philip."

"Oh, but darling," Catherine laughed, "you're forgetting that Evan thinks you and some nameless man tinkered with the bridge. Hillary I've ruined before, and I can ruin him again. As for Philip, he, too, has become a terrible nuisance. No, Philip's days have come to an end."

Cecilia's throat constricted with terror. She staggered backward, her eyes drawn up to the portrait of Lady Eleanora. Suddenly Cecilia realized where she had seen Catherine before. The glacial blue eyes, the thin menacing mouth, the taut self-assured pose of the face—Catherine was all but the woman's double! And with her wearing the open-chested red gown as she was now, her hair piled uncharacteristically on top of her head, it was a simple step to imagine Catherine with the jet black hair of Lady Eleanora. The two could not have looked more alike had they been sisters.

Catherine's cruel laugh made Cecilia jump. She stared into Catherine's eyes uneasily.

"She was very beautiful, wasn't she?" Catherine smirked. "And your stunning piece of detective work—however belated, poor Cecilia—should make it easy for you to see what happens next."

"Catherine," Cecilia breathed in horror, "you're not going to murder Philip?"

"Indeed I am," Catherine rejoined. "And you're going to help me."

Desperately Cecilia fought for air. The green silk scarf around her neck suddenly felt like a noose. She had to stop Catherine.

"You'll never get away with it," Cecilia cried. "They all know what you are, Catherine."

"Not everyone, dear girl. Only the weak ones. Evan is my trump card. Now that he thinks the worst of you, you're doomed to die unmourned. With you, we shall bury any evidence that could implicate me or Mathias."

"No, Catherine!" Cecilia screamed. "You don't understand!"

"I understand perfectly." Catherine's voice was hard and low. "Now, stop screaming. I'm not interested in receiving any visitors at this moment. But be certain that if I have to I'll shoot." She tossed a set of keys at Cecilia's feet, then added, "I couldn't let you run away with any of these precious trinkets in the display cases, now, could I?" Catherine smiled briefly, then her expression hardened. "Open the far case," she ordered.

Cecilia felt faint. She could not bring herself to assist in anyone's murder.

"Now!" Catherine demanded. "Open the far case and take out the bottle of strychnine. Your fingerprints will be most appreciated."

Cecilia thought of charging Catherine, but she knew she would be powerless to outrace the bullet. An idea quickly formed in her mind.

Carefully she bent to pick up the keys. With trembling hands she selected the key she knew would unlock the deadly case. If only her plan could work, Catherine would be thrown off guard. Then Cecilia might win precious seconds in which to take possession of the revolver.

"Drop the bottle, Cecilia, and you'll eat the strychnine up off the floor yourself," Catherine warned.

Cecilia's heart sank. Catherine was a step ahead of her. The case clicked open. She would have to follow each of Catherine's directions until just the right moment. Her only hope lay in playing along until she could see a chance to resist. She could do nothing if she forced Catherine to fire.

With both hands Cecilia lifted the centuries-old vial of poison. She couldn't steady her tremors. Slowly she moved the bottle through the air so that she could set it down on the adjoining case. Her heart skipped a beat as she imagined herself consuming the lethal crystalline drug, but she managed to place the container safely on the next glass-topped case.

"Very good," Catherine crooned. "Now I'll be able to comfort my poor dear Philip with a warming snifter of brandy. Don't you think that would be nice of me, considering the grief I've caused him today?" Her strident laugh left no room for reply.

Cecilia was breathing very heavily now. Time was against her. Catherine had got what she wanted. It only remained to be seen what she would do with Cecilia. The answer was quick in coming.

"Now, move over toward that far wall," Catherine instructed, motioning for Cecilia to move in the direction of the barrel of the revolver. "That's right," she encouraged as Cecilia began to back into the smooth paneled wall. "Stop right at the spot where you found me that lovely day we had our first chat."

Cecilia's teeth began to chatter. She felt chills running up her arms and legs, yet the heat of the hot summer day made her feel damp all over with fear. She knew what that spot on the wall meant.

"Look carefully, at the paneling just behind you," Catherine went on. "You'll see that there's a seam in the wood; four seams, in fact. To your right, about level with your knee, you'll notice a cluster of knots—

three, I think. Press the spot just below the cluster."

Cecilia whirled around. Her options had run out. Her only hope now lay in convincing Catherine there was no hope of escape, that Evan and Hillary would avenge her death—and Philip's too.

"Catherine!" she cried desperately. "Listen to me. Last night I saw Evan. We talked about everything—all the acts of sabotage you and Mathias have carried out, your scheme to discredit Hillary; even the scene in the salon yesterday evening—it was all planned to trick *you*, Catherine! Stop before you add any more serious crimes to the list," she pleaded.

Catherine studied Cecilia seriously for a moment, then her face twisted back into an ugly look of amusement. "You're almost convincing, Cecilia," she replied, "but not quite. Now spring that panel and let yourself slip quietly into the darkness. Mathias will find you later. You'll probably be unconscious from the fall, though. A simple way to die, I should think."

Cecilia knew she had failed. Catherine had completely lost her senses. Cecilia had two choices: face death now from Catherine's bullet, or later at the hands of Mathias.

The panel snapped open when she pressed the spot below the three knots in the wood. She edged into the darkness, choosing to prolong her life, if only for seconds.

Chapter 13

How fatally she had underestimated Catherine! The words kept ringing in her ears. Everyone had underestimated Catherine.

Cecilia couldn't guess how late it was, but she knew it was too late. There was no way of telling how long she had been unconscious. Blackness completely surrounded her. She had fallen instantly when she let herself slip through the trapdoor. She must have lost consciousness the moment she hit the back wall of the shaft, she realized.

As far as Cecilia could tell, she had no broken bones, though her body ached. But what did it matter? She should have seen the inevitable; Catherine was a highly skilled manipulator. Cecilia had no doubt that while Evan slept and Hillary and Emily rediscovered happiness, Catherine had succeeded in murdering the defenseless Philip. She pictured Philip taking the proffered crystal snifter, sadly but willingly. She could see

Catherine kneel in false supplication at his side, watching Philip quaff the last drink of his life.

Cecilia shivered. She felt cramped and ill. There was nowhere to go. She'd felt around in the darkness the moment she'd come to, but the trapdoor led only to this chute—and she had fallen to the bottom. The air in the tiny compartment was thick and suffocating, heavy with an unhealthy dampness and the smell of mold.

Fear suddenly assaulted her again. She had unconsciously refrained from thinking about what lay ahead for her. She was imagining where everyone else might be, but none of her speculations included her own rescue. No, the only hand she could hope to feel was that of Mathias. And she expected no mercy.

A noise sounded. Cecilia was certain she'd heard it. Was someone leaning against one of the walls that formed this passage? Had it been wood creaking?

Cecilia pulled her knees up to her chest. She was defenseless. Someone must be approaching, but how and from where? The sound of breathing followed by a rush of air to her left sent her senses reeling. There was a connecting passageway! She buried her face in her knees.

A flashlight directed at her eyes temporarily blinded her. "Who is it?" she screamed, wishing she'd had the courage to remain silent, to make Mathias come to her. She would fight him off as long as she could, she vowed.

"Evan," came the reply. "And Nick."

Cecilia peered through the darkness. It sounded like Evan. Then the flashlight came on again, but this time it illuminated first Evan's face and next the black-bearded face of Nick. All at once the tension flowed out of her.

She was safe! In the seconds before she fell back against the boards she thought, *I almost died here, but Evan came . . . Evan came.*

THE SUNLIGHT felt more blessed than Cecilia could ever have imagined. She had regained consciousness briefly as Nick had carried her through the passage. Now, as she stepped out of the tunnel into the light, her eyes opened again. They were in the garden. She felt the lush grass brush her legs as Nick laid her down, then she saw Evan's face. A mixture of terrible grief and intense relief showed in his strong features.

"The passage," Evan began softly, "leads underground out through the garden. That chute is designed to break your fall several times before you hit ground, so you'll be very sore for a while. I had to bring Nick with me to rescue you. My arm . . . I wish I could have carried you myself."

Hot tears of relief rolled down Cecilia's cheeks. She felt more wonderful than she had ever felt in her life, cradled tenderly in the curve of Evan's uninjured arm.

"Oh, Evan," she murmured, "Thank God you came. Mathias—"

"Shush," Evan whispered. "I know. We'd all agreed to guard Catherine in the event she tried to escape. Unfortunately Philip couldn't be trusted. . . . I went to look for him as soon as I woke up."

"Philip?" Cecilia inquired hopefully.

Evan shook his head grimly. "You know what Catherine had planned. She succeeded before I could get to them. I simply under—"

"—estimated Catherine," Cecilia sighed.

Evan nodded sadly. "It was too late. But Catherine was still on the scene, and I . . . I literally shook her until she told me where you were. Nick had come by to see how I was and to tell me he'd got the men who were at Hathaway last night. I knew that Tony was helping Gwen in the kitchen—he still doesn't know what happened—and I told him to find Hillary." Evan paused and smiled at Cecilia's flushed face. "That little spy had already seen Hillary and Emily kissing down near the stables, and he was bubbling with happiness at seeing them together again. I sent him to get Hillary, and he returned in minutes with both Emily and Hillary.

"Hillary's called the police by now . . . and an ambulance to take away Philip. He'll be buried here on the estate." Evan paused and his jaw tightened. "Catherine and Mathias, I hope, will live a long time in prison."

Cecilia was filled with a rush of conflicting emotions. She felt warm and content in Evan's arms. And she was happy to hear that Emily and Hillary were really back together. But the thought of what had happened to Philip made her tears flow anew. At least Catherine and Mathias would be punished, though that was small comfort to her. A man had been murdered, and there was no way of giving him back his life.

"What about Tony?" Cecilia cried suddenly.

"That depends partly on you," Evan answered.

"Of course, I'll be with you when you tell him," Cecilia offered at once.

"And after that?"

"After . . . ?"

"Don't you think you've earned yourself a promotion in the tour business?" Evan said tenderly. "I'd like to make you too busy to take the visitors through the place yourself. But maybe you could find the time to supervise them . . . between looking after Tony and . . . ."

"And?" Cecilia asked softly.

"And me," was Evan's reply. "Will you be my wife, Cecilia? I love you more than—"

"Oh, I love you, too," Cecilia cried. "And I want nothing more in life than to be your wife. And to have Tony here with us at Chesterton. And to—"

"And to give us a child of our own?"

Heedless of the bruises and scrapes that covered her body, Cecilia sat up on the grass. She threw her arms around Evan's neck, remembering somewhere in the deep recesses of her mind not to disturb his wounded shoulder. The kiss they shared was free from danger— the danger that had been with them since they'd first met.

What readers say about Mystique Books...

"Each one is better than the one before."
—E.R.,* Milwaukee, Wisconsin

"A hint of mystique adds plenty of spice."
—E.O'D., Belvedere, Illinois

"I thoroughly enjoy them."
—Mrs. B.B., Parma, Ohio

"Mystiques are really great."
—Mrs. A.S., Brussels, Ontario

"You can't put them down once you start reading them."
—Mrs. H.M.,* Marion, Wisconsin

"I like them."
—J.K., Indianapolis, Indiana

"Undoubtedly the best novels I have ever read."
—D.M., Brooklyn, Michigan

"They're great. All characters are mature, sympathetic. Really readable."
—Mrs. W.L.T., Jacksonville, Florida

*Names available on request.

MYSTIQUE BOOKS

Experience the warmth of love...
and the threat of danger!

MYSTIQUE BOOKS are a breathless blend of romance and suspense, passion and mystery. Let them take you on journeys to exotic lands—the sunny Caribbean, the enchantment of Paris, the sinister streets of Istanbul.

MYSTIQUE BOOKS

An unforgettable reading experience.
Now... many previously published titles are once again available.
Choose from this great selection!

Don't miss any of these thrilling novels of love and adventure!

Choose from this list of exciting
MYSTIQUE BOOKS

Experience the excitement of romantic suspense.
MYSTIQUE BOOKS

COMPLETE AND MAIL THIS COUPON TODAY!

MYSTIQUE BOOKS

In the U.S.A.	In Canada
1440 South Priest Drive	649 Ontario Street
Tempe, AZ 85281	Stratford, Ontario N5A 6W2

Please send me the following MYSTIQUE BOOKS. I am enclosing my check or money order for $1.50 for each novel ordered, plus 75¢ to cover postage and handling.

☐ 33	☐ 36	☐ 39	☐ 42
☐ 34	☐ 37	☐ 40	☐ 43
☐ 35	☐ 38	☐ 41	☐ 44

Number of novels checked @ $1.50 each = $ _____

N.Y. and Ariz. residents add appropriate sales tax $ _____

Postage and handling $ _____ .75

TOTAL $ _____

I enclose _____
(Please send check or money order. We cannot be responsible for cash sent through the mail.)

NAME _____
        (Please Print)

ADDRESS _____

CITY _____

STATE/PROV. _____

POSTAL CODE _____